Agatha Christie

Death on the Nile

Collins

Collins

HarperCollins Publishers
The News Building
1 London Bridge Street
London SE1 9GF

www.collinselt.com

Collins® is a registered trademark of HarperCollins Publishers Limited.

This *Collins English Readers* edition first published by HarperCollins Publishers 2017.

10 9 8 7 6 5 4 3 2 1

First published in Great Britain by Collins 1937

www.agathachristie.com

ISBN: 978-0-00-824968-7

A catalogue record for this book is available from the British Library.

Cover design © HarperCollins*Publishers* Ltd/Agatha Christie Ltd 2017

Typeset by Davidson Publishing Solutions, Glasgow

Printed and bound by CPI Group (UK) Ltd., Croydon, CR0 4YY

Contents

Introduction   IV

Story   1

Character list   82

Cultural notes   83

Glossary   86

♦ INTRODUCTION ♦

ABOUT COLLINS ENGLISH READERS

Collins English Readers have been created for readers worldwide whose first language is not English. The stories are carefully graded to ensure that you, the reader, will both enjoy and benefit from your reading experience.

Words which are above the required reading level are underlined the first time they appear in a story. All underlined words are defined in the **Glossary** at the back of the book. Books at levels 1 and 2 take their definitions from the *Collins COBUILD Essential English Dictionary*, and books at levels 3 and above from the *Collins COBUILD Advanced English Dictionary*. Where appropriate, definitions are simplified for level and context.

Alongside the glossary, a **Character list** is provided to help the reader identify who is who, and how they are connected to each other. **Cultural notes** explain historical, cultural and other references. **Maps and diagrams** are provided where appropriate. A **downloadable recording** is also available of the full story. To access the audio, go to www.collinselt.com/eltreadersaudio. The password is the third word on page 52 of this book.

To support both teachers and learners, additional materials are available online at www.collinselt.com/readers. These include a **Plot synopsis** and **classroom activities** (both for teachers), **Student activities**, a **level checker** and much more.

About Agatha Christie

Agatha Christie (1890–1976) is known throughout the world as the Queen of Crime. She is the most widely published and translated author of all time and in any language; only the Bible and Shakespeare have sold more copies.

Agatha Christie's first novel was published in 1920. It featured Hercule Poirot, the Belgian detective who has become the most popular detective in crime fiction since Sherlock Holmes.

Collins has published Agatha Christie since 1926.

The Grading Scheme

The Collins COBUILD Grading Scheme has been created using the most up-to-date language usage information available today. Each level is guided by a comprehensive grammar and vocabulary framework, ensuring that the series will perfectly match readers' abilities.

		CEF band	Pages	Word count	Headwords
Level 1	elementary	A2	64	5,000–8,000	approx. 700
Level 2	pre-intermediate	A2–B1	80	8,000–11,000	approx. 900
Level 3	intermediate	B1	96	11,000–20,000	approx. 1,300
Level 4	upper-intermediate	B2	112-128	15,000–26,000	approx. 1,700
Level 5	upper-intermediate+	B2+	128+	22,000–30,000	approx. 2,200
Level 6	advanced	C1	144+	28,000+	2,500+
Level 7	advanced+	C2	160+	*varied*	*varied*

For more information on the Collins COBUILD Grading Scheme go to www.collinselt.com/readers/gradingscheme.

THE KARNAK
PROMENADE DECK

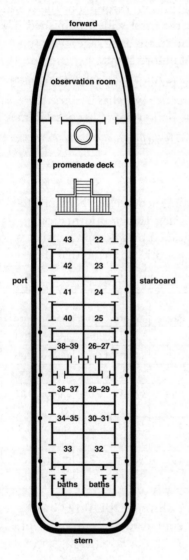

BOAT

CABINS

'Oh Linnet, I think this house is going to be *marvellous!*' The Honourable[1] Joanna Southwood was in Linnet Ridgeway's bedroom at Wode Hall[2].

From the window you could see the beautiful gardens and, in the distance, woodlands.

'It's perfect, isn't it?' said Linnet.

Her face was excited, alive. Beside her, Joanna, a thin young woman of twenty-seven, seemed a little uninteresting. She picked up a <u>pearl</u> necklace.

'They are beautiful. What *are* they worth?'

'About fifty thousand pounds.'

'Can I wear them till dinner time? Please say yes.'

Linnet laughed. 'Of course.'

'Linnet, you really have got *everything.* You're twenty, with lots of money, good looks, perfect health. Tell me, are you going to marry Lord Windlesham?'

'I don't really want to marry *anyone* yet.'

The telephone rang. Linnet answered. 'Yes? *Jackie, how wonderful!* We haven't spoken for *ages!* Can you come down to see my new house? I'd love to show you around.'

'Actually, Linnet, I would love to come to see you,' the voice on the other end of the phone said with excitement.

'Well, jump into a train or a car. Come now!'

'Okay, I will, my sweet. See you very soon.'

Linnet hung up the phone and said to Joanna, 'That's my great friend, Jacqueline de Bellefort. Her parents lost all their money, so Jackie's got nothing. I want to help her, but she won't let me. She's awfully proud and can get very angry about things.

She once stuck a small knife into a boy who was being cruel to a dog. There was the *most* terrible argument!'

Linnet's maid[3] entered; she took a dress from the wardrobe and went out.

'What's the matter with Marie?' asked Joanna. 'She's been crying.'

'She wanted to marry a man who has a job in Egypt. I had to make sure he was a good man. Unfortunately, I found out that he already has a wife – and three children.'

'Oh dear. You must make a lot of enemies, Linnet.'

Linnet laughed. 'Oh no, I don't have a single enemy in the world!'

◆ ◆ ◆

It was four o'clock when a rather old little car arrived. A girl got out – she was very attractive with lots of dark hair.

Linnet was waiting.

'Jackie! What have you been doing all these months?'

'Working. Ugly work with ugly women! I'm here to ask a great big favour! *I'm engaged!* His name's Simon Doyle. He's wonderful! He's poor and he loves the countryside. And I shall *die* if I can't marry him!'

'My <u>darling</u>, *you are in love!*'

'I know.' Jackie's dark eyes looked sad suddenly. 'It's... frightening sometimes! And you must help us, Linnet. Now that you've bought this place, you'll have to have a land agent[2]; I want you to give the job to Simon. He knows all about estates[2] – he grew up on one. Oh, you will give him a job, won't you, beautiful Linnet? Say you will!'

Linnet started to laugh.

'Oh, Jackie! Bring your young man here and let me meet him.'

Jackie kissed her happily.

'*Oh, darling Linnet!* I knew you wouldn't <u>let me down</u> – ever!'

♦ ◆ ♦

Gaston Blondin was the French owner of the famous restaurant, Chez Ma Tante. It was extremely rare for him to greet a guest and accompany him to a special table.

On this night, however, Monsieur Blondin was accompanying a little man with a huge black moustache.

'There is *always* a table for *you*, Monsieur Poirot! Do you have serious crimes to <u>investigate</u>?'

'No – I am a man of leisure. I am trying to enjoy life without work. This winter I will visit Egypt.'

'Ah! Egypt,' repeated Monsieur Blondin.

The orchestra began to play and everybody danced.

Hercule Poirot looked around. How bored most of the faces were! One couple interested him – a tall man with broad shoulders dancing with a slim, attractive girl. They didn't look bored. They moved together in happiness. The dance stopped and the couple returned to their table near Poirot.

The girl was laughing, but there was something besides happiness in her eyes. Hercule Poirot <u>shook his head</u>.

'She cares too much for him,' he thought to himself. 'It is not safe.'

Then he heard a word in their conversation. Egypt.

'I'm *not* being <u>silly</u>, Simon. Linnet won't let us down! It's the right job for you. We'll wait three months and—'

'And then I'll marry you—'

'Yes, and we'll go to Egypt for our honeymoon. The Nile, the Pyramids[4]… But I wonder, do you care about me as much as I care about you?'

Her eyes opened wide, almost with fear.

'Jackie – you *are* being silly.'

But the girl repeated: 'I wonder…'

Hercule Poirot said to himself: 'Yes, I wonder too.'

◆ ◆ ◆

Joanna Southwood and Linnet were talking. Joanna said: 'What if Simon's terrible?'

'Oh, he won't be. I trust Jackie. Now, I must go and look at the plans for my new swimming pool. Some old cottages will have to be destroyed to make space for it. I'm moving the people who live there to new homes.'

'Are the people who live in the cottages happy about their new houses?'

'Well, there are one or two who don't seem to realize how much better their new homes will be!'

Joanna laughed.

'You are awful!'

'I am not!' replied Linnet.

'You always do what you want. If you can't buy something with cash, you buy it with a smile. You don't let anything or anyone stop you. I really do wonder what will happen when someone does try to stop you.'

'Don't be silly, Joanna.'

They heard the sound of a car through the open window.

Jackie and her young man had arrived. Linnet hurried out to meet them.

'Linnet!' Jackie ran towards her. 'This is Simon. Simon, here's Linnet, the most wonderful person in the world.'

Linnet saw a very attractive young man with a very attractive smile…

As he shook her hand, a wonderful feeling ran through her body. She thought: 'I like Jackie's young man… I like him a lot…' And then she suddenly felt sad: 'Lucky Jackie…'

CHAPTER 2

In his New York office, lawyer Andrew Pennington looked up from the letter he was reading for the second time.

He said to his partner: 'Linnet has got married...'

'*What?*' Sterndale Rockford was shocked. Then he said, 'Well, what are we going to do about it?'

'The *Normandie* sails today. One of us could go.'

'Surely you don't want to go over to England to speak to her British lawyers!'

'No, no. Linnet's going to Egypt for her honeymoon. She's planning to be there for at least a month...' said Pennington.

'If I go there, I think there might be ways of... managing the problem,' he added. 'A meeting by chance... Linnet and her husband... A honeymoon atmosphere... It might be possible...'

Pennington looked serious. 'I hope I can do it.'

His partner said: 'You've got to...'

♦ ◆ ♦

Mrs Allerton and her son were sitting outside the Cataract Hotel in Aswan[4] watching a short man dressed in a white silk suit walking with a tall slim girl.

'That's Hercule Poirot, the detective,' said Mrs Allerton with great excitement.

Tim Allerton sat up, more interested than usual. 'That funny little man? And he seems to have attracted the best-looking girl in the place. Pity she looks so <u>bad-tempered</u>.'

Poirot, meanwhile, was walking and talking happily with Rosalie Otterbourne: 'I do like it here very much. The black rocks of Elephantine[4], the little boats on the river.'

'Do you? I think Aswan's dark and sad,' replied Rosalie. 'The hotel's half empty, and everyone's about a hundred!'

Poirot's eyes laughed.

'It is true, I am very old.'

'I – I wasn't thinking of you. I'm sorry. That sounded rude.'

'Not at all. It is natural that you wish to meet people of your own age. Ah, well, there is *one* young man, at least.'

'The one who sits with his mother all the time? I think he looks <u>conceited</u>!'

Poirot smiled.

'My best friend says that I am very conceited.'

'Oh, well, you have something to be conceited about. Unfortunately for you, crime doesn't interest me at all.'

'I am delighted that you obviously have no <u>guilty secrets</u> to hide.'

She glanced at him quickly. Poirot didn't seem to notice, and he carried on talking.

'Madame, your mother was not at lunch today. Is Mrs Otterbourne ill?'

'No, but this place isn't good for her,' said Rosalie. 'I'll be glad when we leave for Wadi Halfa⁴.'

They came to the dusty road by the river. One of the Nile <u>steamers</u> had just arrived and Poirot and Rosalie looked at the passengers.

'Quite a lot of people, aren't there?' said Rosalie.

She turned her head away as Tim Allerton joined them.

'Look!' said Tim with excitement. 'Isn't that Linnet Ridgeway coming off the boat? The tall man's her new husband, I suppose.'

'Simon Doyle,' said Rosalie. 'It was in all the newspapers. She's very rich, isn't she?'

'Very' agreed Tim, happily.

Poirot said quietly, 'She is beautiful.'

'Some people have everything,' said Rosalie angrily.

Linnet Doyle turned to speak to the man by her side. As he answered, Poirot recognized the voice. But where from? He tried to remember.

'It isn't fair,' said Rosalie, so quietly that Tim did not hear.

Tim said, 'I must collect some things for my mother.' And he left.

'So it is not fair, Mademoiselle?' asked Poirot gently.

The girl blushed.

'It just seems too much for one person. Money, good looks, marvellous figure and—'

She paused.

'And love? Eh? But you do not know – maybe he married her for her money!'

'Didn't you see how he looked at her?'

'My dear, I saw something that you did not. I saw dark lines under a woman's eyes, a hand that held a parasol so tight that her fingers were white... There is *something* that is not right. And I wish I could remember where I have heard Monsieur Doyle's voice before.'

Rosalie said angrily: 'I'd like to put my foot on her conceited face. I'm a jealous cat and I just hate her! I've never hated anyone so much immediately!'

Poirot shook her arm in a friendly way.

'Magnificent! You will feel better because you have said that!'

Rosalie laughed.

'Good, there we are,' said Poirot, and laughed too.

They walked happily back to the hotel.

'I must find Mother,' said Rosalie.

So Poirot went into the gardens alone.

There, he saw the girl from Chez Ma Tante. She was paler now, with thin sad lines on her face.

A face and a voice! Suddenly, Poirot remembered them both. Monsieur Doyle was with this girl that night in the restaurant. And now, it seemed, he was married to someone else.

The girl got quickly to her feet as Linnet Doyle and her husband came down the path.

'Hello, Linnet,' said Jacqueline de Bellefort. Linnet Doyle stepped back with a cry.

'We seem to meet each other everywhere,' continued Jacqueline.

Simon Doyle was very angry. Poirot thought he might hit the girl.

Jacqueline turned her head a little towards Poirot to show Simon that he was watching.

Simon stopped himself quickly and said simply: 'Hello, Jacqueline... We didn't expect to see you here.'

Jacqueline turned and walked slowly up the path towards the hotel. Poirot heard Linnet Doyle say: 'Simon, what can we do?'

CHAPTER 3

The <u>terrace</u> outside the Cataract Hotel looked down on the Nile. After dinner, most of the guests were sitting at little tables enjoying the night air.

Simon and Linnet Doyle came outside, accompanied by a smart grey-haired man. Tim Allerton rose from his chair and approached them. 'You probably don't remember me,' he said to Linnet, 'but I'm Joanna Southwood's cousin. We've met before.'

'Oh, of course,' replied Linnet. 'You're Tim Allerton. This is my husband, Simon, and this is my American <u>trustee</u>, Mr Pennington.'

Tim shook hands with the two men, then said: 'You must meet my mother.'

A few minutes later, they were all sitting together when Poirot came out onto the terrace. Before he could choose a table for himself, Mrs Otterbourne called to him: 'Join me, Monsieur Poirot.' So he did, smiling politely. What a silly hat she was wearing!

'Quite a lot of interesting people here now, aren't there?' she said. 'The young, rich and beautiful, famous writers—' She paused with a laugh.

'Are you writing a book at the moment, Madame?'

'No, but I really must begin. My readers are waiting! Have you read my books?'

'Sadly, Madame, I—'

'I must give you a copy of *Under the Apple Tree*.' She looked quickly from side to side. 'I'll get it for you.'

'What is it, Mother?'

Her daughter, Rosalie, was suddenly at her side.

'Nothing. I was just going to get a book for Monsieur Poirot.'

'*Under the Apple Tree*? I'll get it,' said Rosalie, and moved quickly across the terrace into the hotel.

'Madame, you have a very lovely daughter,' said Poirot.

'Rosalie?' said Mrs Otterbourne. 'She doesn't understand how I feel at all. She doesn't care about my – my illness. She imagines she knows more about my health than I do—'

'A drink, Madame?'

Mrs Otterbourne shook her head.

'No, I hardly ever drink alcohol.'

'Then a lemonade, Madame?'

As he gave the order, Rosalie came towards them, a book in her hand.

'Here you are,' she said.

Poirot took the book and read the information on the back cover. It said how wonderful this realistic story of a modern woman's love life was.

Poirot's eyes met Rosalie's. The look in her eyes made him feel sad.

The three sat in silence.

Just at that moment, the door to the terrace opened again and Jacqueline de Bellefort appeared.

She sat down at an empty table and looked across at Linnet Doyle – who stood up suddenly and went into the hotel.

Jacqueline smiled to herself and looked out over the Nile.

CHAPTER 4

'Monsieur Poirot?'

Poirot had stayed on the terrace after everyone else had left. Now, Linnet Doyle had come back.

'Monsieur Poirot,' she repeated, 'I know who you are, and I need your help.' Giving him no time to refuse, she continued:

'Before I met my husband, he was engaged to a Miss de Bellefort, a friend of mine. My husband ended it – he didn't love her. She made threats which thankfully she has not attempted to do anything about. But now we're on our honeymoon and she's following us everywhere we go. We saw her first in Venice. Then we found her on board the boat at Brindisi. When we got here, she – she was waiting. This has got to stop!'

'Madame, if a young lady wishes to travel to various places, and you and your husband are, by chance, in those same places – what can we do?'

'But it is unacceptable!'

'*Ecoutez* – listen, Madame,' said Poirot calmly. 'A little story. One day, a month or two ago, I am eating in a restaurant. At the table next to me are a man and a woman. The man's back is facing me, but I can see the woman's face. She is completely in love. They are engaged to be married, and they talk of their honeymoon. They plan to go to Egypt.

'I know that I will remember the woman's face. And I remember the man's voice. And here in Egypt I see the face and hear the voice again. The man is on his honeymoon, yes – but *with a different woman*. The woman in the restaurant mentioned a friend who she was certain would not let her down. That friend, I think, was you, Madame.'

Linnet blushed. 'Monsieur Poirot, you think that I stole my friend's man. But although Jackie was completely in love with

Simon, even before he met me he was starting to feel that it was a mistake. I'm very sorry about it, but he was going to end it anyway.'

'I wonder,' said Poirot. 'To you, your friend being here is *unacceptable* – and why? Because *you feel guilty.* I suggest that you chose to take your husband away from your friend. I suggest that you wanted him from the moment you met him. But there was a second when you <u>hesitated</u>. The decision was yours – not Monsieur Doyle's. That is why seeing Mademoiselle de Bellefort everywhere is making you unhappy. You believe you may be wrong and she may be right.

'I think, Madame, that you have had a happy life, that you have been generous and kind to others.'

'I have tried to be.'

Linnet spoke almost sadly.

'And that is why the feeling that you have hurt someone makes you so upset,' said Poirot.

'Even if what you say is true,' said Linnet, 'we must all <u>accept</u> things as they are. Why can't Jackie?'

Poirot <u>nodded</u>.

'Yes, we must accept things as they are. And sometimes, we must also accept the <u>consequences</u> of what we have done.'

'Monsieur Poirot, couldn't you talk to Jackie?' asked Linnet. 'Persuade her to go home?'

'I do not believe that anything I say will persuade Mademoiselle de Bellefort. You said she has made threats. Will you tell me what those threats are?'

'She made threats to – well – to kill us both.'

'I see,' Poirot said in a serious voice.

'So will you talk to her? For me?'

'I will talk to her, Madame,' said Poirot, 'But not for you. I will do it for her, and for all of us. But I am not hopeful.'

CHAPTER 5

Poirot found Jacqueline de Bellefort sitting on the rocks next to the river.

'Mademoiselle de Bellefort, may I join you?'

'Shall I guess?' she said. 'Mrs Doyle has promised you a large fee and has asked you to come and speak to me.'

'Yes and no,' he said, smiling. 'I am not accepting a fee. I sat next to you once at Chez Ma Tante. You were there with Monsieur Doyle.' A strange look appeared on Jacqueline's face.

'Mademoiselle,' continued Poirot, 'What is done is done. Go home. You are young – you could do anything in the world.'

'You don't understand – *Simon* is my world. You saw us in the restaurant that night… You know that Simon and I loved each other. All her life Linnet has been able to buy everything she wanted. She wanted Simon – so she just took him.'

'And he allowed himself to be taken?'

'Linnet is much more attractive and exciting than I am, Monsieur Poirot. And money helps that.' She suddenly pointed into the night sky. 'Look at the moon. You can see it clearly now. But if the sun was shining, you wouldn't be able to see the moon at all. It was rather like that. I was the moon… When the sun came out, Simon couldn't see anything but… Linnet. She made him fall in love with her. But he did love me – he will always love me.'

'Even now?'

Her face was a deep red colour.

'I know, he hates me now… He'd better be careful.'

She felt in her little silk bag, then held out her hand. In it was a small gun decorated with pearl. 'Look, I bought this when Simon left me. I was going to kill him or Linnet, but I couldn't decide which one. Then I had this idea, to follow them! And it's worked! It's spoiling everything for both of them.'

She laughed. Poirot touched her arm.

'Mademoiselle, I ask you, please – do not do this. Do not open your heart to <u>evil</u>. Because, if you do, *evil will make its home inside you*.'

For a moment, he thought she might agree. Then she cried: 'No, you can't stop me. Even if I want to kill her, you can't stop me.'

'No… not if you understand the consequences of murder[5].' His voice was sad.

Jacqueline de Bellefort laughed again.

'Oh, I'm not afraid of death! I have no reason to live now, anyway. Sometimes I want to put my little gun against her head and then just press with my finger… *Oh*!'

'What is it, Mademoiselle?'

She was looking into the dark trees near them. 'Someone was watching us. He's gone now.'

Poirot looked round quickly but saw nothing.

'I see no one here but us, Mademoiselle.' He stood up. 'Well, I have said all I came to say. Good night.'

Jacqueline said quickly: 'You understand that I can't do what you're asking, don't you?'

Poirot shook his head.

'No, you could do it!' He spoke quietly and seriously. 'There was a moment in which your friend Linnet could have stopped herself… She let that moment pass. And if you let your moment pass too, you won't get a second chance.'

CHAPTER 6

The next morning Simon Doyle joined Hercule Poirot to walk down to the town.

'Have you talked to Jackie? Did you persuade her to go home?'

'I am afraid not, Monsieur Doyle.'

'I admit that what I did to her was not very nice, but I'd understand better if she did something like trying to shoot me. Following us is making Linnet feel very guilty. But I've got a plan. I've announced that we're going to stay here for ten days. But tomorrow the *Karnak* sails from Shellal[4] to Wadi Halfa. I'm going to book us tickets for that boat using <u>false</u> names. Tomorrow we'll go on a trip and join the *Karnak* at Shellal. By the time Jackie realizes we haven't come back, we'll be far away and she won't be able to find us.'

'That is an interesting plan,' replied Poirot. 'I will be on the *Karnak* too. It is part of my tour.'

'Well, then you must tell us something about your detective <u>cases</u> one evening. Your work is rather exciting. Mrs Allerton thinks so and she'll also be coming on the *Karnak*.'

'Does she know about your plans?' asked Poirot.

'Certainly not. It's better not to trust anybody.'

'Yes, I agree.'

Poirot continued: 'And the tall grey-haired man... Who is he?'

'Pennington – Linnet's American trustee. We met him by chance in Cairo.'

'I see. Is your wife twenty-one yet?'

'No, not yet. She wrote Pennington a letter soon after we were married to tell him, but he left New York on the *Carmanic* two days before the letter arrived. So he didn't know anything about it until he met us in Cairo – he was very surprised!'

'And your wife has not told Monsieur Pennington about this trouble with Mademoiselle de Bellefort?'

'No. Besides, when we met Pennington and started this Nile trip, we thought it was all finished.'

'No,' said Poirot, 'it is not all finished – I am very sure of that.'

◆ ◆ ◆

Poirot decided to spend the rest of the morning on the island of Elephantine, so he walked down to the hotel's private jetty.

There, already getting into one of the hotel boats, were two men, obviously strangers to each other. The younger was a dark-haired young man, lost in his own thoughts, wearing very dirty grey trousers. The other was a middle-aged Italian who introduced himself to Poirot as Signor Guido Richetti, Archaeologist.

They reached Elephantine quickly, with the Italian – now speaking to Poirot in French – chatting all the way. When they arrived, Poirot saw a familiar face down by the river, so he escaped in that direction.

He joined Mrs Allerton sitting on a rock.

'Good morning, Monsieur Poirot,' she said happily. They chatted for a few minutes before Mrs Allerton said, 'I saw you with Simon Doyle this morning. Do tell me what you think of him! One of our relatives, Joanna Southwood, is one of his wife Linnet's best friends.'

'Ah, she is much in the news, Mademoiselle Southwood.'

'Oh, she knows how to advertise herself,' Mrs Allerton said. 'I don't like her – Tim and she are the best of friends, though.'

Changing the subject, Mrs Allerton continued: 'Tim tells me that dark-haired girl used to be engaged to Simon Doyle. She almost frightened me last night on the terrace, she looked so serious.'

'Yes, strong feeling is always frightening,' agreed Poirot.

'Do ordinary people interest you too, Monsieur Poirot? Or are you interested only in people who might turn into criminals?'

'Madame, there are not many people outside that group.' He added: 'Mothers, for example, can be particularly dangerous when their children are in danger.'

'Yes, you're quite right.' Mrs Allerton stood up and began collecting her things.

'We must be getting back. The *Karnak* sails immediately after lunch.'

When they reached the jetty, the young man with the dirty grey trousers was already waiting in the boat. Poirot said politely:

'There are so many wonderful things to see in Egypt, are there not?'

'I hate them all,' the young man replied angrily. 'Think of the Pyramids. Huge pieces of useless stone built to make a few rich kings feel important. Think of the people who died building them. Human beings matter more than stones.'

'But they do not last as well,' Poirot replied.

Signor Richetti had now joined them and clearly did not like the young man's views.

'I'd rather see a happy, healthy worker than any great work of art. We must think about the future, not the past,' continued the young man. Richetti got angrier and angrier, shouting at him in Italian.

The young man then spent the whole journey telling everybody exactly what he thought of the awful <u>capitalist</u> system.

As they finally reached the hotel, Mrs Allerton said happily: 'Well, well,' which obviously succeeded in annoying the young man even more.

◆ ◆ ◆

After lunch, the hotel bus took the passengers visiting the Second Cataract[4] to the train station for the journey to Shellal. From there they were going to travel on the *Karnak*, a small steamer.

On the train, there was an elderly lady who looked like she disliked most of the world. A rather nervous young woman was sitting opposite her. From time to time the old lady shouted at her for no obvious reason.

'Poor girl,' thought Poirot. 'I wonder why she accepts it.'

On the *Karnak*, most of the passengers had accommodation on the promenade <u>deck</u>. The whole forward part of that deck was a large observation room. On the deck below were a smoking room and a large room for sitting and relaxing. On the deck below that was the dining room.

Poirot joined Rosalie Otterbourne outside on the promenade deck to watch the departure.

'So now we go into Nubia[4],' said Poirot.

'Yes. Don't you think that there's something about Egypt that brings all the feelings that are boiling inside you to the top? I feel everything's so unfair. Look at – at some people's mothers and look at mine.' She stopped suddenly and looked embarrassed. 'I – I shouldn't say things like that.'

'Why not? If you are boiling inside, you have to let the bad feelings come to the top and then you can remove them, like so.' He moved his hand as if dropping something into the Nile. 'Then, they have gone.'

'What an extraordinary man you are!' Her bad-tempered mouth suddenly smiled. 'Oh look, here are Mrs Doyle and her husband! I didn't know *they* were coming on this trip!'

Linnet had just come out of a cabin with Simon. They looked happy.

Behind them they heard a laugh. Linnet turned round quickly.

Jacqueline de Bellefort was standing there.

◆ ◆ ◆

Some hours later, the *Karnak* was moving quickly down the river.

Poirot was standing on the observation deck when Linnet Doyle appeared next to him.

'Monsieur Poirot, I'm afraid. What's going to happen? I've always been nice to people, I've never had an enemy, but now... I feel surrounded by enemies. I feel that Simon is my only friend. It's terrible to feel that there are people who hate you. We're caught here. There's no way out...'

Poirot felt sorry for her.

She bit her lip.

'I'm sorry, Monsieur Poirot. I'm being silly. I must change my dress for dinner.' And she was gone.

CHAPTER 7

Mrs Allerton, in a simple black evening dress, went to the dining room with her son.

'By the way, I asked Hercule Poirot to sit at our table.'

'Mother, you didn't!' Tim sounded annoyed.

Mrs Allerton wondered why. Tim was usually so easy-going. As they sat down, Poirot came in.

Mrs Allerton wanted them all to enjoy their dinner together. She picked up the passenger list beside her plate.

'Let's try and name everybody,' she said happily. 'Now, Miss de Bellefort is at the same table as the Otterbournes. Who comes next? Dr Bessner?' She looked at a table at which four men sat. 'I think he might be the fat one with the moustache. He's Austrian, I heard. Mr Fanthorp is next – he must be the quiet young man who never speaks, sitting at that same table. He's intelligent, I think.'

Poirot agreed.

'Yes. He listens carefully and he also watches.'

'Mr Ferguson,' read Mrs Allerton, continuing down the list. 'He must be our friend who dislikes the capitalist system. Mr Pennington we know – I'm sure he must be very rich. Mr Richetti – our Italian archaeologist.

'Now, Miss Bowers, Miss Robson and Miss Van Schuyler. Miss Van Schuyler is the very ugly old American lady who was on the train with you. The two women with her must be Miss Bowers and Miss Robson. Perhaps the thin one is a secretary, and the other one – the young woman, who is obviously enjoying herself in spite of being used like a <u>slave</u> – may be a poor relation. But which is Bowers and which is Robson, I wonder…?'

Mrs Allerton was greatly enjoying her own game.

After dinner Poirot spent his evening listening to Mrs Otterbourne talk about being a writer.

On his way to his cabin, he found Jacqueline de Bellefort out on the deck. She looked very sad.

She said: 'Are you surprised to find me here?'

'Not so much surprised as sorry.'

She threw her head back.

'Ah, well, everyone must follow their own star – wherever it leads.'

'Be careful, Mademoiselle, that it is not a false star...'

Later, Poirot was nearly asleep when he heard Simon Doyle's voice outside.

'We can't stop now...'

'No,' thought Hercule Poirot, 'we cannot stop now...'

He was not happy – not happy at all.

Chapter 8

Next morning, at Ez-Zebua[4], Cornelia Robson was the first to hurry off the boat with Hercule Poirot. As they walked up a wide, straight road, she answered happily when he said: 'Are your friends not coming to see the <u>temple</u>?'

'Well, Cousin Marie – that's Miss Van Schuyler – has to be careful of her health. Miss Bowers is her nurse. But she was very kind and said it was all right for me to come.'

'Very kind of her,' said Poirot.

'Oh, Cousin Marie *is* very kind. It was she who suggested to Mother that I came on this whole trip with her – we've been everywhere.'

'You are a very happy person, Mademoiselle.'

He looked from her to the unhappy Rosalie, who was walking by herself.

'She's very pretty, isn't she?' said Cornelia. 'But she looks like she thinks she's better than everyone else.'

After the tour, they returned to the boat. The *Karnak* continued its journey up the river. The scenery was less dusty now. There were trees and crops growing.

Linnet seemed almost happy.

Andrew Pennington said to her: 'I hate to talk business, but some time I need your signature on several documents.'

'Let's do it now, then,' suggested Linnet.

Pennington glanced round. The only people in the observation room were Mr Ferguson, Monsieur Poirot, and Miss Van Schuyler.

'That's fine,' he said, and he left to get the documents. Linnet and Simon smiled at each other.

'All right, sweet?' he asked her.

'Yes... It's funny, I'm not worried any more.'

Pennington came back.

'OK, this one is for the house in New York, so...'

Jim Fanthorp came into the room and took a seat nearby.

'... your signature there,' Pennington said.

Linnet picked up the document, read it quickly, then signed.

Pennington showed her another document.

'This is nothing important,' said Pennington. 'You don't need to read it.'

'I always read *everything*,' said Linnet. 'Father taught me that.'

'She's much more careful than I would be,' said Simon. 'I just sign where they tell me to.'

To everyone's surprise, silent Mr Fanthorp spoke to Linnet.

'You must let me say how clever I think you are. I am a lawyer – and never to sign a document unless you have read it first, is *very* sensible.'

Then, red in the face, he turned to look at the Nile.

Simon Doyle could not decide if he should be annoyed or not.

'Next, please,' said Linnet, but Pennington shook his head.

'If you're going to read everything, we'll be here for hours. We can do this later.'

Poirot moved out onto the deck. As he passed round the back of the boat he almost ran into a young, dark-haired woman who had been talking to a big man in uniform. They both looked guilty. Poirot wondered what they had been talking about.

He came around the stern and Mrs Otterbourne nearly fell into his arms.

'I'm so sorry,' she apologized. 'The boat keeps moving, you know...'

Poirot smiled at her, nodded his head and walked on.

♦ ◆ ♦

On Monday morning the steamer stopped at Abu Simbel[4], a great temple <u>carved</u> into the rock with four huge statues at its entrance.

'Amazing, isn't it?' said Simon Doyle. 'I'm so glad we came on this trip. Linnet's feeling better again. She says she's being positive now.'

'Yes,' said Poirot, thinking.

They got off the boat and went into the temple, where they divided into groups.

Dr Bessner read in German from his guide book, translating for Cornelia Robson who walked beside him. Miss Van Schuyler was holding Miss Bowers' arm. She called Cornelia over and Dr Bessner smiled at her as she walked away.

'A very nice girl,' he announced to Poirot. 'She listens very intelligently.'

The group was now deep inside the temple, in a room where four more huge statues sat.

Simon said suddenly to Linnet: 'Let's get out of here. I don't like these four – they're too realistic. Come outside with me.'

Linnet laughed, but followed him.

They sat with their backs to the <u>cliff</u>.

'How lovely the sun is,' thought Linnet. 'How warm, how safe…'

Her eyes closed.

Simon's eyes were open. What a fool he'd been to be worried that first night… After all, you could trust Jackie—

Suddenly there was a shout, people waving their arms… Simon jumped up and pulled Linnet out of the way as a huge rock rolled down the hill, passing exactly where she had been sitting seconds earlier. Poirot and Tim Allerton were just coming out of the temple and saw the whole thing. They ran to the Doyles.

'Oh, Madame, that was lucky!' Poirot said, shocked.

All four looked up at the cliff where the rock had fallen from. They couldn't see anyone or anything strange. But there was a path along the top – Poirot remembered seeing some Egyptians walking along it earlier.

'Jacqueline!' Simon shouted.

Poirot said quickly: 'Come back to the boat, Madame. You must rest.'

As they reached the boat, Simon suddenly stopped.

Jacqueline de Bellefort was walking towards them, just coming off the boat.

Simon grabbed Poirot's arm. 'Oh! I thought—'

Poirot nodded his head.

He turned and noted where everyone else was.

Miss Van Schuyler was returning to the boat with Miss Bowers.

A little further away, Mrs Allerton was standing with Mrs Otterbourne.

He couldn't see the others. Poirot shook his head as he boarded the boat.

CHAPTER 9

The *Karnak* arrived at Wadi Halfa that night. The next morning, two small boats took all the passengers to the Second Cataract, except for Signor Richetti, who insisted on going somewhere on his own.

Mrs Allerton and Poirot were walking up to the rock above the Second Cataract. Most of the others had gone up on camels.

Miss Van Schuyler had stayed on the boat. 'I'm sorry that you have to stay with me, Miss Bowers,' she said, 'but Cornelia left without saying a word. *And* I saw her talking to that awful young man, Ferguson.'

'I'm happy to stay, Miss Van Schuyler.' Miss Bowers looked up at the hill. 'Cornelia is with Dr Bessner now.'

Miss Van Schuyler thought she could accept this. She had discovered that Dr Bessner had a <u>reputation</u> as a fashionable doctor and, therefore, she liked him.

When everyone returned to the *Karnak,* Linnet gave a cry of surprise.

'A message for me!'

She quickly tore it open. 'I don't understand – potatoes, carrots—'

An angry voice said: 'That message is for *me*.' Signor Richetti took it from her hand.

Linnet turned over the envelope.

'Oh, what a fool I am! It's Richetti – not Ridgeway. I am sorry, Signor Richetti. You see, my name was Ridgeway before I married, and so—'

'It is very bad to be careless like this.' He went out angrily.

Linnet said angrily to Simon, 'These Italians are really awful.'

'Never mind, darling; let's go and look at that souvenir you liked.'

They left the boat together.

Behind him, Poirot heard someone breathing. He turned to see Jacqueline de Bellefort.

She spoke quietly, so only Poirot could hear. 'I don't worry them any more. I can't hurt them... But they will *not* be happy together – I'd rather kill him than...'

As she turned away from him, Poirot felt a hand on his other shoulder.

'Your friend seems a little upset, Monsieur Poirot.'

Poirot turned.

'<u>Colonel</u> Race!'

The year before, the two men had met at a dinner party that had, unfortunately, ended in a death. Race was not a policeman – he was a member of one of the British Government's secret intelligence units[6]. When there was trouble, Race was usually there.

'I'm going with you to Shellal,' explained Race.

'I think you would get there quicker on the Government steamer, which travels by night as well as day...' said Poirot, thinking. 'So, I suppose that you are here for the passengers...?'

'One of the passengers,' agreed Race.

'Which?' Poirot asked.

'I don't know. He's guilty of five or six murders and is one of the cleverest paid criminals ever... He's on this boat. I know that from a letter that said: "X will be on the *Karnak* trip February seventh to thirteenth."'

'Do you have a description?'

'No. Have you got any ideas?'

'An idea, yes – but it is not enough to speak of,' said Poirot.

Race knew Hercule Poirot didn't say anything unless he was sure.

Poirot said unhappily: 'There is something else on this boat that I am worried about. A person A has done something bad to a person B. Now person B has made threats.'

'Are A and B both on this boat?'

'Yes. And yesterday person A was nearly killed, but B could not have done it – B was not there. It might have been an accident, but I do not like accidents. If I am right, and I am always right' – Race smiled – 'then we should be worried. I hope that we arrive at Shellal without a great disaster.'

CHAPTER 10

It was the evening of the next day; the *Karnak* was at Abu Simbel again. In the observation room Miss Van Schuyler was talking to Dr Bessner when Cornelia came in.

'I hope I haven't been too long, Cousin Marie,' Cornelia said.

'What have you done with my <u>velvet</u> <u>shawl</u>?' the old woman asked angrily. 'I had it in here.'

Jim Fanthorp helped Cornelia look for the shawl, but they couldn't find it. So Miss Van Schuyler, Miss Bowers and Cornelia left, with Miss Van Schuyler still shouting at Cornelia.

It was still quite early, but most people had already gone to bed. The Doyles were playing cards with Pennington and Race, and Hercule Poirot was sitting near the door, feeling very tired.

As Poirot went out onto the deck, Jacqueline de Bellefort almost bumped into him.

'Pardon, Mademoiselle.'

'You look sleepy, Monsieur Poirot.'

'*Mais oui* – Yes, it has been a very long day.'

'Yes. The sort of day when things – break! When everything is just too much...' Her voice sounded upset. She hurried off. 'Good night, Monsieur Poirot.'

Poirot wondered what she had been talking about. Confused and worried, he went to his room.

Later, Cornelia went back to the observation room. The four card players were still there, while Fanthorp was reading a book.

Suddenly Jacqueline de Bellefort came in. She walked across to Cornelia, and sat down.

The barman came. Jacqueline ordered a drink. When it came, she said: 'Well, here's to crime,' drank it, and ordered another.

Linnet stood up.

'I think I'll go to bed.'

'Me too,' said Colonel Race.

'Yes,' agreed Pennington. 'Are you coming, Simon?'

'Not yet. I'll have a drink first.'

Linnet left and the others followed. Only Jim Fanthorp and Cornelia Robson were left with Simon and Jacqueline.

Cornelia began to stand up too.

'Don't go, Miss Robson,' said Jacqueline. 'I feel like talking.'

'You need to go to bed, Jackie,' said Simon.

She began to laugh. 'Simon is afraid I'm going to tell you the story of my life, Miss Robson. You see, he did a very bad thing to me, didn't you, Simon?'

Jim Fanthorp shut his book, glanced at his watch, stood up and walked out. It was obvious to everyone why he was leaving.

Jacqueline said: 'I told you that I'd rather kill you than see you with another woman... You're *mine*!'

Jacqueline's hand was searching for something under the table.

'You're mine...' she repeated. Her hand found a small gun and pointed it at Simon.

He jumped to his feet as she pulled the <u>trigger</u>. He fell across a chair. Cornelia screamed and ran to the door. She called out to Jim Fanthorp who was outside.

'Mr Fanthorp! She – she's shot him!'

Simon Doyle lay exactly where he had fallen. Jacqueline stood, shocked, looking at the blood slowly coming through Simon's trouser leg just below the knee. He held a <u>handkerchief</u> against it.

'I didn't mean... Oh, I didn't really mean...' Jacqueline cried.

She dropped the gun onto the floor and kicked it away. It went under one of the sofas.

Simon, his voice weak, said: 'Fanthorp, there's someone coming… Say it's all right… Don't let anyone see.'

A crew member came to the door. Fanthorp said: 'It's all right – we're just having fun!'

The man nodded his head and went away.

Fanthorp turned back.

'I don't think anybody else heard. It only sounded like someone opening a bottle of champagne.'

Jacqueline began to cry.

'Oh, no, what have I done?'

Cornelia hurried to her. 'Ssh, dear. Ssh.'

Simon, pain on his face, said urgently: 'Look, take Jackie to her cabin, Fanthorp. Miss Robson, tell that nurse, Miss Bowers, to stay with her – don't leave her alone. Then find Dr Bessner and bring him here. And make sure my wife doesn't hear about this.'

Between them, Fanthorp and Cornelia took Jacqueline to her cabin.

She was still crying.

'I'll throw myself into the Nile! Oh, Simon – Simon!'

Fanthorp said to Cornelia: 'You get Miss Bowers. I'll stay here.'

When Cornelia returned a few minutes later with the efficient Miss Bowers, Fanthorp hurried to Dr Bessner's cabin. The doctor picked up a little case and accompanied Fanthorp back to the observation room.

Simon had managed to get the window beside him open for air, but his face was now a terrible colour.

The doctor looked at his leg.

'Yes, it is bad... The bone is broken. Mr Fanthorp, we need to take him to my cabin.'

As they lifted him, Cornelia appeared at the door. Fanthorp was beginning to look very sick.

'Come, Miss Robson,' said the doctor. 'I need help. You aren't scared of blood, are you?'

'No, I'm not. I can help,' said Cornelia, quickly taking Fanthorp's place by the patient.

For the next ten minutes, there was a lot of blood.

'Well, that's the best I can do,' announced Dr Bessner at last. 'I'll give you something to make you sleep.'

As he was going to sleep, Simon said: 'You mustn't blame Jackie...'

Then he said: 'Fanthorp, the gun... It's still there...'

'I'll go and get it now,' and Fanthorp left to find the gun.

Three minutes later there was a knock on Dr Bessner's door.

'Dr Bessner?' Fanthorp called him out onto the deck. 'I can't find that gun...'

CHAPTER 11

The next morning, Hercule Poirot was washing his face when Colonel Race entered his cabin.

'Linnet Doyle's dead – shot through the head last night,' said the Colonel. Poirot was silent, thinking about everything that had happened. He did not, however, look shocked.

'They've put me in charge,' continued Race. 'The boat will be stopped for now. There's a possibility, of course, that the murderer was not a passenger on the boat with us.'

Poirot shook his head. 'No,' he said. 'It is definitely one of the passengers.'

'You're probably correct. Well, this has to be your case, Poirot.'

'I am very happy to help,' said Poirot.

There were four cabins with private bathrooms on the boat. The first on the port side was Dr Bessner's, and the other was Andrew Pennington's. On the starboard side, the first was Miss Van Schuyler's, and the one next to it was Linnet Doyle's. A crew member opened Mrs Doyle's cabin door for them. Dr Bessner was already there.

'What can you tell us, Doctor?'

'Well, she was shot just above the ear. A little <u>bullet</u> from a small gun, I think. The gun was held against her head – the skin is burnt. She didn't know anything about it. The murderer entered in the dark and shot her when she was sleeping.'

Poirot thought this explanation was very unlikely. Jacqueline de Bellefort coming into a dark cabin, with her gun in her hand? No, she would never behave like that.

Looking around the room, Poirot saw that on the white wall in front of him someone had drawn very badly a big letter J in red.

Poirot gently picked up the dead girl's right hand. One finger had red on it.

'Mmm – so, Madame Doyle is dying; she writes with her finger, in her own blood, the first letter of her murderer's name. Oh, yes, it has been done so often – in crime stories!'

Bessner cried: 'The poor lady died immediately. To put her finger in the blood (and there is hardly any) and write the letter J on the wall? Oh no, it isn't possible!'

'Why 'J'?' Race asked.

'Jacqueline de Bellefort,' explained Poirot. 'A young lady who told me that she wanted "to put my little gun against her head and then just press…"'

There was a silence. Then Race said: 'What about time of death?'

Bessner thought for a moment.

'She has been dead certainly six hours, probably not longer than eight.'

'So she was shot between midnight and 2 am. What about her husband? Does he sleep in the cabin next door?'

'Yes, but at the moment he's asleep in my cabin,' explained the doctor. 'Mr Doyle was also shot last night, in the observation room.'

'Shot? Who by?' asked Poirot and Race, shocked.

'By Jacqueline de Bellefort.'

'Is he badly hurt?' asked Poirot.

'Yes, I'm afraid he is,' replied Bessner.

Race said: 'Let's go somewhere private. There's a smoking room on the deck below.'

In the smoking room they discussed the murder further. 'It's very clear what happened,' said Race. 'The girl shot Mr Doyle. Then she went along to Linnet Doyle's cabin and shot her as well.'

'No, no. It's *impossible* that Miss de Bellefort shot Mrs Doyle.' The doctor was certain.

Bessner explained that Miss Bowers was with Jacqueline.

'And I'm sure that Miss Bowers stayed with her all night.'

Poirot asked: 'Who found Linnet Doyle?'

'Her maid, Louise Bourget, when she went to wake her as usual,' said Race.

He continued: 'Well, I don't think we need to keep you here any longer, doctor,' and Bessner left.

'Well, Poirot?' Race asked. 'What shall we do next?'

'First of all, we must question Mr Fanthorp and Miss Robson. The missing gun is important.'

Race sent a crew member to get them. While they waited, Poirot shook his head.

'This is bad.'

'You think that this girl Jacqueline does not have the ability to plan a <u>cold-blooded</u> murder,' guessed Race.

'She has the brains,' said Poirot, thinking, 'but I am not sure that she could actually *do* it.'

The door opened and Fanthorp and Cornelia came in. They explained what they had seen. Poirot said: 'So Mademoiselle de Bellefort has an <u>alibi</u> – she had no opportunity to go and get her gun. Monsieur Fanthorp, what time was it when you went to look for it?'

'Just before half past twelve.'

'And how long was it from the time you and Dr Bessner carried Monsieur Doyle out of the observation room until you returned for the gun?'

'Five minutes, or perhaps a little more.'

'So, the person who removed the gun was probably Madame Doyle's murderer. That person had heard or seen the events that took place with Monsieur Doyle and Mademoiselle de Bellefort. The gun was hidden under the sofa, so it is clear that it was taken by *someone who knew it was there.*'

Jim Fanthorp shook his head.

'I didn't see anyone when I went out onto the deck just before the gun was fired. No one was watching from the deck.'

'Yes, but you went out onto the starboard side. You would not have seen anybody at the port door looking through the window.

'Before you go, Monsieur Fanthorp,' continued Poirot, 'please tell me – why are you visiting Egypt?'

Fanthorp paused, then said: 'Er – for pleasure.'

'Ah!' said Poirot. 'And one more question. Did you hear anything – anything at all – after you went to your cabin?'

'Actually, I think I heard a <u>splash</u> just as I was falling asleep. At about one o'clock.'

Fanthorp left and Poirot turned to Cornelia.

'Mademoiselle Robson, your cabin is on the other side of the boat.

'Yes, next door to Miss de Bellefort.'

'Did you hear a splash?'

'No, but I wouldn't, because the boat's against the jetty on my side.'

'Thank you. Now please ask Mademoiselle Bowers to come here.'

◆ ◆ ◆

Miss Bowers gave her name, address, and qualifications.

'Is Mademoiselle Van Schuyler's health very bad?' asked Poirot.

'Oh, no. She just likes plenty of attention, and she's happy to pay for it.'

Poirot said: 'Please can you tell me exactly what happened last night?'

'Well, Miss de Bellefort was very shocked. I gave her some pills, she fell asleep and I sat with her until this morning.'

Jacqueline de Bellefort was definitely not the murderer.

Who, then, had shot Linnet Doyle?

CHAPTER 12

Jacqueline de Bellefort entered. She was very pale.

'I didn't do it! Oh, please believe me. I nearly killed Simon last night – I was mad, I think! But I didn't kill Linnet.'

She began to cry. Poirot gently touched her shoulder.

'There, there. We *know* that you did not kill Madame Doyle.'

Race said: 'Excuse me – I just thought of something,' and he hurried out.

Jacqueline de Bellefort continued: 'Death's horrible! I hate the thought of it. I – I wanted her dead, and now she *is* dead. And she died just like I said – it's awful! I was right, that night at the hotel. There *was* someone listening!'

Poirot nodded his head. 'Yes, Madame Doyle was killed exactly as you described.'

'That man – who was he?'

'Are you sure it was a man?'

She thought for a minute.

'Well, it was really just a – a shadow...'

Bessner appeared. 'Mr Doyle would like to speak to you, Monsieur Poirot.'

Poirot left the room with the doctor. Race joined them. They went up to Bessner's cabin.

Simon Doyle looked terrible.

'The doctor told – told me about Linnet...' He paused. 'But I wanted to tell you – Jackie wouldn't do cold-blooded murder!'

Poirot said: 'Do not be upset. It was not Mademoiselle de Bellefort, but can you give us any idea of who it might have been? Your wife told me that she felt surrounded by enemies.'

'A name on the passenger list made her upset.'

'What name?'

'She didn't tell me,' replied Simon. 'She just said that someone's father had lost money because of her father.'

Bessner said: 'Ferguson spoke against Mrs Doyle once or twice, because she was so rich.'

Turning again to Mr Doyle, Poirot asked, 'Did Madame Doyle have any valuable jewellery with her?'

'There was her pearl necklace...' said Simon.

Next, they interviewed Mrs Doyle's maid, Louise Bourget. Simon Doyle was with them. Louise Bourget was the dark-haired French woman Poirot had seen with the man in a uniform. She had been crying, but there was a strange look on her face.

'When did you last see Madame Doyle alive?'

'Last night, Monsieur. I was in her cabin to undress her.'

'What time was that?'

'After eleven, Monsieur. I put her to bed, and then I left.'

'How long did that take?'

'Ten minutes, Monsieur.'

'And when you left her, what did you do?'

'I went to my own cabin.'

'And you heard or saw nothing that can help us?'

'Monsieur, I was on the deck below, and my cabin is on the other side of the boat. *If* I had been unable to sleep, *if* I had climbed the stairs, *then* perhaps I might have seen the murderer enter or leave Madame's cabin, but—'

She opened her hands to Simon. 'Monsieur, what can I say?'

'My good girl,' said Simon quickly, 'I'll look after you. Nobody's saying you did anything wrong.'

'Monsieur is very good.'

'And you don't know of anyone who hated Mrs Doyle, do you?' asked Race.

'Oh yes, I do. Madame Doyle's maid before me, Marie – she was going to marry one of the crew members on this boat. Fleetwood is his name. But Madame Doyle discovered that he has a wife here in Egypt. And so Marie refused to see Fleetwood any more. He told me that he would like to kill Madame Doyle!'

'Did you say anything to Mrs Doyle about this?' asked Race.

'Of course not.'

Changing the subject, Poirot asked: 'Do you know anything about Mrs Doyle's pearl necklace?'

'She was wearing it last night.'

'Where did she put it when she went to bed?'

'On the table, the same as always.'

'Did you see it this morning?'

'I did not even look. I saw Madame, and then I screamed and ran out of the door.'

Poirot understood.

'You did not look. But I have eyes which notice, and there was *no pearl necklace on the table this morning.*'

CHAPTER 13

Poirot recognized Fleetwood as the man he had seen talking to Louise Bourget.

Race said: 'Mrs Doyle has been murdered. We know that she stopped her maid from marrying you.'

Fleetwood was angry. 'It wasn't her business! I *was* angry with her, especially when I saw her on this boat, all dressed up in pearls, not even thinking about what she'd done to me. But I didn't touch her!'

'Where were you last night between the hours of twelve and two?'

'In my cabin, asleep – I share a room, so my friend will tell you that's true.'

'The next thing, I think,' said Race, 'is to find out if anyone heard anything which might tell us the time of the crime. Let's start on the starboard side. Let's speak to the Allertons.'

Mrs Allerton came in, clearly upset.

'It's horrible,' she said. 'But I'm so glad you're here. You'll be able to find out who did it. I'm so glad it wasn't that poor girl.'

'You mean Mademoiselle de Bellefort,' said Poirot. 'Who told you she did not do it?'

'Cornelia Robson,' said Mrs Allerton, with a small smile. 'But you want to ask me some questions.'

'Yes, please. What time did you go to bed, Madame?'

'Just after half past ten.'

'And did you hear anything at all during the night?'

'I think I heard a splash and someone running – or was it the other way round?'

'Do you know what time that was?'

'No, but I don't think it was long after I fell asleep.'

'Had you ever met Madame Doyle before this trip?'

'No, but Tim had. And I'd heard about her from Joanna Southwood.'

'I have one other question, if you will excuse me for asking. Did you, or your family, ever lose any money because of Madame Doyle's father?'

Mrs Allerton was surprised.

'Oh, no! My husband left me very little money, but I still have all of it. Though it doesn't help so much these days...'

Poirot repeated his questions to Tim Allerton.

'I went to bed early, at about half past ten, and I read for a while,' said Tim. 'I put out my light just after eleven. I heard somebody calling Fanthorp, then a lot of different voices. And then somebody running along the deck. And then I heard something – a splash?'

'Are you sure it was not a *gun* you heard?' asked Poirot.

'It might have been... I did hear a champagne bottle – or that's what I thought. I remember thinking there was a party going on. And I wished they'd all go to bed and be quiet!'

Marie Van Schuyler was not happy about Poirot's questions.

Poirot said gently: 'Mademoiselle, you went to bed last night at what time?'

'Ten o'clock is my usual time. Last night I was a little later. I was waiting for Cornelia.'

'And did you hear anything after you had gone to bed?'

'Yes, I heard Mrs Doyle's maid saying goodnight to her in a voice that was far louder than necessary. I fell asleep again and woke thinking someone was in my cabin, but it was someone in Mrs Doyle's cabin next door. Then I heard someone on the deck and a splash. I looked at my clock. It was ten minutes past one.'

'And you have no idea what made the splash?'

'Oh yes, I know – I went to my door to see. Miss Otterbourne had dropped something into the water.'

'Rosalie Otterbourne?' Race sounded surprised. 'And then?'

'Miss Otterbourne went away round the stern and I returned to bed.'

There was a knock at the door and a crew member entered. He carried a wet velvet package.

'We've got it, Colonel.'

He passed the package to Race, who opened it. A cheap handkerchief fell out, <u>stained</u> pink, wrapped round a small gun decorated with pearl.

'So it *was* thrown into the river.' Race looked at the gun. 'Two bullets were fired.'

'And that is my shawl!' said Miss Van Schuyler. 'I was asking *everyone* if they'd seen it.'

There were burns and small holes in the shawl.

'The murderer wrapped your shawl round the gun to stop the noise, Mademoiselle Van Schuyler.'

'Well, really!' Miss Van Schuyler walked out. Race and Poirot looked at each other.

'Rosalie Otterbourne? I didn't expect that,' Race said.

Poirot hit the table with his hand. 'No! *The order of events is impossible.* Something is wrong.'

Colonel Race respected Hercule Poirot's brain.

'What next? Shall we ask the Otterbourne girl some questions?'

'Yes.'

Rosalie Otterbourne didn't look frightened, but she did look in a bad mood.

'Well? What is it?' she asked.

Poirot said: 'Did you leave your cabin last night? Did you go round to the starboard side of the boat and throw something into the river?'

She blushed red.

'No, I didn't.'

'Miss Van Schuyler says she saw you throw something into the water.'

Rosalie was now very pale.

'You see, Mademoiselle, something *was* thrown into the river last night,' said Poirot.

Race held out the velvet shawl and its contents.

'Is that – what she was killed with?' asked Rosalie.

'Yes, Mademoiselle.'

'But why would I want to kill Linnet Doyle? It really wasn't me Miss Van Schuyler saw. Can I go now?'

Race nodded and Rosalie Otterbourne left. 'Well, which of them do we believe?'

Poirot shook his head.

'Actually, I have a feeling that they are both lying.'

Mrs Otterbourne also said that she and Rosalie had gone to bed before eleven. She had heard nothing, and didn't know if Rosalie had left their cabin or not. However, she had a lot to say on the subject of the crime.

'That girl Jacqueline, angry and jealous, a silent murderer, gun in hand—'

'But Jacqueline de Bellefort did not shoot Madame Doyle,' explained Poirot. 'That is a fact.'

Disappointed, Mrs Otterbourne then tried to blame several other people in a variety of ways.

Clearly, Mrs Otterbourne had no more information for them. Colonel Race opened the door for her.

'What an awful woman! Now, who have we got left? Let's keep Pennington until the end. Richetti, then Ferguson, I think. Both have cabins on the lower deck on the starboard side.'

Signor Richetti had turned out his light some time before eleven. The only thing he had heard was a big splash.

'One, two, three hours after I went to sleep. I'm not sure. Oh, what a terrible crime...'

Signor Richetti went out, waving his hands around at how terrible it was.

Ferguson said. 'Does it really matter? There are so many unnecessary rich women in the world! I did hear something like a champagne bottle, people running about on the deck above. And I believe I did hear a splash. But I'm not sure.'

'Did you leave your cabin during the night?'

Ferguson smiled.

'No, I didn't.'

CHAPTER 14

Andrew Pennington said he'd heard and seen nothing.

Poirot said: 'You were the dead woman's lawyer in America, her trustee, and a close family friend. You would know, perhaps, if there was a reason why someone would want her dead?'

'Well no, I have no idea...'

Colonel Race said: 'Mr Doyle mentioned someone being on the *Karnak* who hated her family. Do you know who that is?'

Pennington looked surprised. 'No.'

'She nearly died when that rock crashed down at Abu Simbel,' continued Poirot. 'Were you there?'

'No, I was inside the temple.'

Pennington touched his hot face with a silk handkerchief.

The interview ended there. Andrew Pennington left the room.

'Mr Pennington,' said Race, 'was not comfortable.'

'And,' Poirot said, 'he lied. He was *not* in the temple when that rock fell. I had just come from there. But, for the moment, let us be very careful with him.'

'Agreed,' said Race.

The boat began to move under their feet. The *Karnak* had started on her journey back to Shellal.

'We need to find that necklace... Here's an idea,' said Race excitedly. 'At the end of lunch, I'll announce that the pearls have been stolen, and I'll ask everyone to stay in the dining room while we search for them.'

Poirot said: 'Excellent. The person who took the pearls still has them. If they do not know about the search, they cannot throw them into the river.'

There was a knock on the door and a crew member entered.

'Excuse me, sir,' he said to Poirot, 'Mr Doyle is asking for you.'

In Bessner's cabin, Simon's face was red with fever.

'I want to see Jackie. She's only a child and I want to apologize...'

Poirot found Jacqueline de Bellefort in a corner of the observation room.

She followed him like a confused child.

When she saw Simon she spoke quickly.

'Simon – I didn't kill Linnet. I didn't! I – I was mad last night. Oh, Simon! I could have killed you!'

'Not with a silly little gun like that...'

Jacqueline sat down by Simon's bed. She was crying. He touched her gently. His eyes met Poirot's and the detective left the cabin.

Poirot paused at the next cabin, thought for a moment, and then knocked.

Rosalie Otterbourne appeared at the door, dark circles under her eyes.

'What do you want?'

'A few minutes' conversation, Mademoiselle.'

She came out, closing the door behind her. 'Well?'

'Let us talk honestly, Mademoiselle. At Aswan I saw immediately that you were protecting your mother from her secret drinking. However, she got some alcohol from somewhere and I think that yesterday you discovered where she was hiding it. So, as soon as your mother was asleep, you went out and threw the bottles into the Nile. Am I right?'

Rosalie was shocked. 'Yes! I didn't want everyone to know. And it seemed so silly that—'

'Anyone would think you are a murderer?'

'Yes! Mother's books stopped selling and she was so upset. And so she began to drink. I always have to watch her...' She paused. 'I'm so very, very tired.'

'I know,' said Poirot.

'Are you – are you going to tell everyone?'

'No, no. Just tell me – at what time was this? Ten minutes past one?'

'Yes, about then.'

'Mademoiselle Van Schuyler saw *you*, but did you see *her*?'

'No. I just looked along the deck and then out to the river.'

'And did you see anyone when you looked along the deck?'

Rosalie paused. At last she shook her head. 'No. I didn't see anybody.'

CHAPTER 15

The mood on the boat was not happy. People came into the dining room very quietly. Tim Allerton arrived after his mother, looking very bad-tempered.

'It's no joke being involved in a murder case. We are *all* suspects. And there's the missing pearl necklace, too.'

'Linnet's pearls? I suppose that was the motive for the crime,' said Mrs Allerton.

'Why do you say that? They're two different things.'

'Who told you that they were missing?'

'Ferguson. A crew member told him.'

Poirot sat down with the Allertons. He ordered a bottle of wine, then said to Tim: 'Tell me, Madame Doyle's cousin, Mademoiselle Joanna Southwood – is she similar to Madame Doyle?'

'You've got it wrong, Monsieur. She's *my* cousin and was Linnet's friend,' explained Tim.

'Ah, excuse me. You see, I have been interested in her for some time.'

'Why?' asked Tim.

Poirot began to stand up as Jacqueline de Bellefort came in, breathing hard. As he sat down again, Poirot seemed to have forgotten Tim's question. He said:

'I wonder if all young ladies with valuable jewellery are as careless as Madame Doyle was.'

'Tim says this will be unpleasant for all of us,' said Mrs Allerton.

'Ah, so you know that someone has taken her pearls! Have you been in a house where something was stolen before?'

'Never,' said Tim.

'Darling, you were at the Portarlingtons' when that woman's jewellery was stolen.'

'No, Mother – I was there when she discovered that the necklace she was wearing was only glass. Her real one was probably taken months earlier. People said she'd done it herself!'

'Joanna said that, did she?' replied Mrs Allerton.

'Joanna wasn't there, Mother.'

'But she knows the Portarlingtons well.'

Poirot quickly changed the subject.

Dessert had been served when Race announced that the pearl necklace was missing and that they were going to do a search of the passengers and their cabins.

Poirot went to Race and spoke in his ear.

Race said a few words to a crew member, then Race and Poirot went out onto the deck.

'Good idea, Poirot,' Race said. 'We'll give them three minutes before we start looking in the cabins.'

Soon, the door opened and the crew member came out. 'You were right, sir. There's a lady who says she needs to speak to you immediately. It's Miss Bowers.'

Race looked surprised.

'Let's talk to her.'

They had just reached the smoking room when the crew member arrived with Miss Bowers.

'Well, Miss Bowers?'

'Colonel Race, I thought the best thing to do was to speak to you immediately.' She opened her neat black handbag. 'To return this.'

She took out a pearl necklace and put it on the table.

'Did *you* take this from Mrs Doyle's cabin?'

'No, Miss Van Schuyler did. She can't help it. That's really why I'm always with her. She takes things. But she always hides them in the same place – wrapped up in a pair of tights – so I look each morning.

'I knew whose they were, of course, and I went to put them back, but a crew member was outside Mrs Doyle's cabin. He told me about the murder and that no one could go in. I've had a very difficult morning wondering what to do.'

'What does Miss Van Schuyler say about this?'

'Oh, she never admits taking anything.'

'Does Miss Robson know?'

'No. Her mother thought it would be best if she didn't know.'

'Well, we have to thank you for coming to us, Mademoiselle,' said Poirot. 'Now tell me, is Mademoiselle Van Schuyler a little deaf?'

'She is, Monsieur Poirot.'

'Would she hear anyone moving about in Mrs Doyle's cabin?'

'Oh, no. Not at all.'

'Thank you, Miss Bowers,' Race said. 'You can go back now and wait with the others.'

He watched her go. Poirot picked up the necklace.

'So, the old lady *did* look out of her cabin and she *did* see Rosalie Otterbourne. But I do not think she *heard* anything. I think she was just looking out before going to steal this pearl necklace.'

'The Otterbourne girl was definitely there, then?'

'Oh, yes. She was throwing her mother's secret drinks away.'

Colonel Race looked surprised. 'I see! And *she* didn't see or hear anything?'

'I asked her that. She answered – after at least a few seconds – that she did not see anybody. The reason she paused means something, I think.'

'Anyway, we should do our search. The necklace still gives us a good excuse,' continued Race.

'Ah, this necklace!' Poirot put it down. 'Actually, I am quite certain that these pearls are false. I admired Madame Doyle's pearls the first evening on the boat – they were wonderful. She was wearing the real ones then – not these.'

'Then we've got to find them,' said Race. 'And hopefully, we will also see which man has cheap handkerchiefs, like the one we found wrapped round the gun.'

Poirot and Race started their search on the lower deck. Signor Richetti's cabin contained two personal letters, and his handkerchiefs were all of coloured silk.

Although Ferguson's clothes were torn and dirty, his handkerchiefs were expensive.

'Some interesting differences,' said Poirot.

Next was Louise Bourget's cabin. The maid had her meals after the other passengers, but Race had asked a crew member to take her to join the others. That crew member met them outside her cabin.

'I'm sorry, sir, but I don't know where the young woman is,' he said.

Poirot and Race decided to return to Louise's cabin later.

They went up to the promenade deck and started on the starboard side. Jim Fanthorp's cabin was very neat. Everything he had was of good quality.

'No letters,' said Poirot. 'He is careful to destroy them.'

Next door in Tim Allerton's cabin, a big <u>rosary</u> was hanging on the wall with wooden <u>beads</u>. There were also some letters. Poirot looked at them quickly. None were from Joanna Southwood.

'No cheap handkerchiefs,' said Race, putting back the contents of a drawer.

Poirot studied a tube of glue for a moment or two, then said: 'Let us continue.'

Mrs Allerton's cabin was so neat that it was perfect. Race said as they left it: 'A nice woman.'

The next cabin was Simon Doyle's. Some of his things had been moved to Bessner's cabin, but many were still there.

'We must look carefully here,' said Poirot. 'It is possible that the thief hid the pearls here, in the cabin of a man *who cannot possibly visit it himself.*'

But there were no pearls.

Then Race took a key and opened the door of Linnet Doyle's cabin.

The cabin was exactly as it had been that morning, except that Linnet's body had been removed.

Poirot noticed two little bottles of <u>nail polish</u>, labelled *Nailex*. He smelled both of them. One, *Nailex Rose*, was empty except for a drop or two of dark red liquid. The other, *Nailex Cardinal*, was nearly full.

Poirot and Race then went into Marie Van Schuyler's cabin, where there was nothing unusual.

The next cabin was Poirot's, and Race's was next to that.

Coming around the stern they searched Miss Bowers' cabin carefully but found nothing. Her handkerchiefs did not match the one they had found with the gun.

The Otterbournes' cabin came next. Here, again, nothing.

The next cabin was Bessner's. Simon Doyle was looking much worse.

Poirot explained what they were doing.

Simon said: 'You don't think old Bessner took them, do you?'

Poirot thought for a moment.

'Well, what do we know about Dr Bessner? Only what he tells us himself.'

But they found nothing.

The next cabin was Pennington's. Poirot and Race carefully looked through a case full of business documents.

Poirot shook his head. 'These all seem to be normal.'

He lifted a heavy gun out of a drawer and put it back.

'I am sure that gun means something,' he said. 'But Linnet Doyle was not shot with it.'

Outside on the deck, Poirot suggested that Race should search the rest of the cabins while he spoke with Simon Doyle.

He went back into Bessner's cabin.

'Tell me, did Madame Doyle ever lend her necklace to Mademoiselle de Bellefort?' he asked.

Simon blushed. 'What are you saying? That Jackie stole the pearls? Jackie is completely honest. The idea of her being a thief is crazy.'

Poirot looked at him with bright eyes.

'*Oh, la! la!* So you have strong feelings about that!'

The door opened and Race came in.

'We haven't found anything,' he said. 'And the crew members are here to report on their search of the passengers.'

Two crew members appeared.

The first said: 'There was no necklace, sir. But the Italian man was quite upset. He had a gun on him, too. A Mauser .25.'

'Italians get angry quickly,' said Simon. 'Richetti got into a very bad mood at Wadi Halfa because of a mistake about a message.'

Race turned to the other crew member.

'There was nothing on any of the ladies, sir. But Miss Otterbourne had a small gun decorated with pearl in her handbag.'

Race looked confused. 'Does every girl on this boat carry a gun?

'What about Mrs Doyle's maid?' asked Poirot.

'We can't find her anywhere.'

'When was she last seen?'

'About half an hour before lunch, sir.'

'Well, let's have a look in her cabin anyway,' said Race.

Louise Bourget's cabin was very messy. There were clothes everywhere.

But her shoes were in a perfect line beside the bed. This was very strange. Race looked down at them. Then he said in a serious voice: 'She hasn't disappeared. *She's here – under the bed…*'

Chapter 16

The two men looked at Louise's dead body.

'She's been <u>stabbed</u> in the heart,' said Race. His voice was very sad.

There was something in the fingers of her right hand. Poirot took it.

'It's the corner of a thousand-franc note[7]. Oh Race, we have been fools! What did she say? "*If* I had climbed the stairs, *then* perhaps I might have seen the murderer—" I realize now – she *did* come up. She *did* see someone.'

'I see! She demanded money to keep quiet,' said Race, 'and the murderer paid her in French money.'

'And while she counted it, the murderer stabbed her, took the money back and ran, not noticing that the corner of one note was torn.'

'We may catch him that way,' said Race.

'I doubt it. He will look at those notes and see the tear.'

Race shook his head, looking sad.

'I'll get Bessner to come down here.'

'She has been dead for less than an hour,' Bessner announced. 'And what did the murderer use to kill her?'

'Something very sharp, very thin. I can show you the kind of thing.'

Back in his cabin he opened a case and took out a doctor's knife. 'Something like this.'

'I suppose,' said Race, 'that none of your own knives are missing, Doctor?'

Bessner's face grew red.

'None! Now, will you please leave? I have to clean my patient's leg.'

Miss Bowers entered as Race and Poirot were leaving. Race walked off and Poirot turned to his left.

He heard a little laugh. Jacqueline and Rosalie were in the Otterbournes' cabin. The door was open and the two girls were standing near it. Rosalie smiled at Poirot.

'We were just comparing make-up.'

There was something strange about Poirot's smile, and Jacqueline de Bellefort saw it.

'What's happened?' she asked.

'I am afraid another death has happened,' said Poirot.

Poirot saw fear in Rosalie's eyes.

'Madame Doyle's maid saw someone enter and leave Linnet Doyle's cabin on the night of the murder – and so she was killed.'

'Did – did she say who she saw?' Rosalie asked.

Poirot shook his head.

Suddenly, Cornelia Robson appeared.

'Oh, Jacqueline, something awful has happened!'

Jacqueline turned to her. Poirot and Rosalie moved off in the other direction along the deck and he said, quietly:

'Mademoiselle, you have not been honest with me. You did not tell me everything you saw last night – or that you carry a small gun in your handbag.'

'What are you talking about?' she said.

She went into her cabin and came back with her handbag.

'Look for yourself.'

There was no gun inside.

'You're not always right, Monsieur Poirot.'

'No? About the gun, perhaps, but I think you saw a man come out of Linnet Doyle's cabin and walk away down the deck and – perhaps – enter *one of the two cabins at the end.* Am I right?'

She bit her lip gently.

'I didn't see anyone,' said Rosalie Otterbourne.

CHAPTER 17

Colonel Race was coming quickly along the deck.

'Poirot! I've got an idea. What Doyle said about a message. It might not be important, but... you never know. Two murders and we're still <u>in the dark</u>.'

Poirot shook his head. 'No, no. We are in the light.'

'Since when?'

'Since the death of Louise Bourget! If I could tell you now, I would. But there is a lot to do first. I knew that the gun being removed from the place of the crime meant something. I only realized what that was half an hour ago. But now let us solve the problem of the message you mentioned.'

They went back into Dr Bessner's cabin. The doctor was still in a very bad mood.

'My patient has a fever.'

'Just one question for Mr Doyle,' said Race.

Dr Bessner pushed past them.

'I will return in three minutes, and then you will leave!'

Simon Doyle looked from Poirot to Race.

'Yes, what is it?' he asked.

'You said that Signor Richetti had been angry,' Race replied, 'About a message. Can you tell me what happened?'

'At Wadi Halfa, Linnet thought she saw a message for her. She'd forgotten that she wasn't called Ridgeway any more. Richetti and Ridgeway do look similar if the handwriting isn't very good, so she opened it. Richetti pulled it out of her hand in a very rude way.'

'And do you know what was in that message?'

'It said—'

Outside there was a lot of noise.

'Where are Monsieur Poirot and Colonel Race? I have some important information,' said a woman's voice.

Bessner had not closed the door. Only the curtain hung across the entrance. Mrs Otterbourne moved it to one side and entered like a powerful storm.

'Mr Doyle,' she began, 'I know who killed your wife!'

Race said quickly: 'Can you *prove* who killed Mrs Doyle?'

'Certainly. I know who killed Louise Bourget – therefore I know who killed Linnet Doyle.'

Simon, confused, ill and excited, shouted: 'Look, start at the beginning. You know the person who killed Louise Bourget, you say.'

'You mean, you *think* you know who killed Louise Bourget,' said Race.

'No, I *saw* the person with my own eyes. On our way to lunch I told Rosalie to go in without me. I had to – er – meet someone.'

The curtain across the door moved a little behind Mrs Otterbourne, but none of the men noticed it.

'One of the crew was – er – getting me something I needed, but I didn't want my daughter to know about it.

'I was meeting him at the stern on the deck below this. As I went, a cabin door opened and Louise Bourget looked out. When she saw it was me, she looked disappointed and went inside again. I went and got the— got what I wanted from the man and turned around to walk back to my cabin – but as I came around the corner I saw someone knock on the maid's door and go into the cabin.'

'And that person was—?'

Bang!

The noise of a gun filled the cabin. Mrs Otterbourne fell to the ground. From behind her ear the blood flowed from a round, neat hole.

There was a moment of terrible silence when nobody could think properly. Then the two men jumped to their feet. Race went to Mrs Otterbourne while Poirot went out of the door.

On the ground lay a big heavy gun.

Poirot glanced in both directions. The deck was empty. He moved as fast as he could towards the stern. As he went round the corner, he met Tim Allerton running towards him.

'What was that?' cried Tim.

'Did you meet anyone on your way here?'

'No.'

'Then come with me.' He took the young man by the arm and went back the way he had come. Rosalie, Jacqueline, and Cornelia had run out of their cabins. More people were coming from the observation room – Ferguson, Jim Fanthorp and Mrs Allerton.

Pointing forward on the boat, Race said: 'He didn't go that way. Fanthorp and Ferguson were sitting in the lounge; they'd have seen him.'

Poirot added, 'And Monsieur Allerton would have met him if he had gone towards the stern.'

Race said, pointing to the gun: 'I think we've seen this before. We must make sure, though.'

He knocked on the door of Pennington's cabin. The cabin was empty but the door was open. Race checked – the gun was gone.

They found Pennington writing letters on the deck below.

'Didn't you hear a gun?' Race asked.

'I did hear a loud noise. But I never thought— Who's been shot?'

'Mrs Otterbourne. With your gun.'

'What? Well, clearly I couldn't have gone to the deck above, killed this poor woman and come down again with no one seeing me.'

'But it was your gun that was used.'

'Well, there was a conversation about guns one evening, and I said that I always carried one with me.'

'Who was there?'

'Most people, I think.'

Poirot said: 'Monsieur Pennington, I would like to discuss some parts of the case with you. Will you come to my cabin in half an hour?'

'I'd be delighted.'

Pennington did not look delighted.

Race and Poirot returned to the place of the murder.

Cornelia, her eyes wide, said: 'How did no one see the murderer leave?'

Jacqueline said: 'Maybe he threw himself over the side and to the deck below.'

'Oh!' said Cornelia, shocked. 'He'd have to be very quick.'

Race said: 'Would you all mind leaving us? We want to bring out the body.'

Everyone moved away, Poirot with them.

Cornelia said: 'Three deaths... It's like living in a nightmare.'

Ferguson said: 'Really? Who will miss *them*? Linnet Doyle and her money! The French maid – trying to get money. Mrs Otterbourne – a useless fool!'

'You're wrong, Mr Ferguson!' Cornelia shouted. 'Mrs Otterbourne's daughter was fond of her. I am sure somebody somewhere was fond of the maid; and as for Linnet Doyle, well, I'm not beautiful myself, and that makes me like beauty in other people. And when anything beautiful dies, the world misses it!'

Mr Ferguson took a step back.

'You're amazing. You haven't got anything bad in you – you are all good.' He turned to Poirot. 'Do you know, sir, that

Cornelia's father lost all his money because of Linnet Ridgeway's father? But does the girl feel angry when she sees the daughter dancing about in a pearl necklace? No, not at all.'

Cornelia blushed. 'I did – just for a minute. But all that was in the past.'

'Cornelia Robson, you're the only nice woman I've ever met,' Ferguson said excitedly. 'Will you marry me?'

'No! You wouldn't be *reliable*,' said Cornelia.

She ran into her cabin.

Ferguson watched her as she left. 'I want that girl.'

He turned and went into the observation room, followed by Poirot.

Ferguson approached Miss Van Schuyler.

'Look, Miss Van Schuyler, your cousin has refused to marry me! But I'm going to keep asking her until she agrees.'

'Then I will do my best to make sure that my young cousin doesn't have to listen to you,' replied Miss Van Schuyler.

'Why don't you like me? I've got two legs, two arms, good health, and an OK brain.'

'There is the problem of your position in society, Mr Ferguson…'

The door opened and Cornelia came in.

Mr Ferguson gave a broad smile. 'Cornelia. Your cousin says I'm not good enough for you. That, of course, is true, but not in the way she means it. Her point is that my social position is too far below yours. Is that why you won't marry me?'

'No, it isn't.' Cornelia blushed. 'If – if I liked you, I'd marry you, but I – I think you're awful. I—'

She ran from the room in tears.

'Well,' said Mr Ferguson, 'that's not too bad a start.' With a cheerful smile he went out of the door.

'I am afraid he is rather a strange man,' said Poirot to Miss Van Schuyler. 'He calls himself Ferguson and he will not use his <u>title</u> because of his political beliefs.'

'His *title*?'

'Yes – Lord Dawlish. He is very rich, and he went to Oxford university.'

'How long have you known this, Monsieur Poirot?'

'There was a picture in one of the papers. Oh, it is true, I promise.'

He enjoyed the confused look on Miss Van Schuyler's face.

CHAPTER 18

Race found Poirot in the observation room.

'Well, Poirot, Pennington should be here in ten minutes.'

Poirot stood up. 'First, would you bring Fanthorp to my cabin?'

Soon, Fanthorp was seated in front of Poirot.

'Now, Monsieur Fanthorp, I notice that you wear the same tie that a friend of mine, Hastings, wears.'

'It's my old school tie from Eton[8],' Fanthorp said.

'Exactly. You went to a good school. You know that there are "things which you may do" and "things which you may not do". One of those things which you may not do is to interrupt a private conversation when you do not know the people who are speaking.

'But the other day *that is exactly what you did*. You sat near to hear the conversation, and you spoke to Madame Doyle about her good business methods.'

Jim Fanthorp's face turned very red.

'You are also a very young man to be able to take an expensive holiday, and a lawyer in a small village company, probably not earning much money. With all of this information, I ask myself: *what is your reason for being on this boat?*'

'I don't want to answer you, Monsieur Poirot. I think you must be mad.'

'I am definitely not. You work in Northampton, not very far from Wode Hall, Madame Doyle's new home. Tell me, why did you speak to Madame Doyle? I believe it was *to stop her from signing any document without reading it first.*'

Poirot continued.

'Madame Otterbourne was killed with a gun owned by Monsieur Andrew Pennington – now perhaps you will realize that you have to tell us why you came on this trip?'

Finally, Fanthorp began to speak. 'I was sent by my uncle, Mr Carmichael, who is Mrs Doyle's English lawyer. He often wrote to Mr Pennington, Mrs Doyle's American trustee. Recently several things made my uncle begin to suspect Pennington...'

'Your uncle believed that Pennington was a criminal?' asked Race.

Jim Fanthorp nodded his head.

'There were conversations which made my uncle think that Pennington was not being honest. But, with Miss Ridgeway's marriage, my uncle believed the problem would be solved – when she returned to England she could take control of the estate Mr Pennington managed.

'However, in a letter she wrote to my uncle from Cairo, she mentioned that she had met Andrew Pennington. He felt sure that Pennington was going to try and get signatures from her which would give him permission for the awful <u>risks</u> he was taking with her money. Since my uncle had no <u>evidence</u>, he decided to send me to Egypt to watch Pennington and do something if necessary. After I spoke to Mrs Doyle when she was signing those documents, I felt sure that Pennington would leave her alone for a while. By then I hoped to know Mr and Mrs Doyle well enough so that they would listen to my warning.'

Poirot asked, 'Monsieur Fanthorp, if you wanted to <u>deceive</u> Madame Doyle or Monsieur Doyle, which one would you choose?'

Fanthorp smiled.

'Mr Doyle, every time.'

'I agree,' said Poirot. He looked at Race. *'And there is the motive.'*

Jim Fanthorp left them. Two minutes later Andrew Pennington arrived.

Poirot began immediately: 'I understand that Mademoiselle Ridgeway would have taken control of all her money in June?'

'Yes.'

'But her marriage changed that and she could have had her money now?'

Pennington's face changed.

'I don't see how this is important.'

Poirot sat forward, his eyes green and cat-like. 'I was wondering, Monsieur Pennington, if Linnet Ridgeway's marriage made you nervous? It all happened very suddenly. Is Linnet Doyle's money where it should be?'

'Yes, it is!'

'So you were not worried when you heard the news about her marriage? You did not race to Europe by the first boat to try to meet her 'by chance' in Egypt?' asked Poirot.

'I didn't even know that Linnet was married until I met her in Cairo. Her letter arrived the day after I left New York.'

'You came over by the *Carmanic*, I think you said. It is strange that on your luggage the only recent labels are from the *Normandie*, which sailed two days *after* the *Carmanic*...'

Pennington was quiet, so Poirot continued: 'Monsieur Pennington, we believe that you came to Egypt to try to delay things. That you tried to get Madame Doyle to sign documents without reading them. But your plan did not work. We also know that when you were walking on the cliff at Abu Simbel, you pushed a rock down the hill which almost killed Madame Doyle.

'We also *know* that it was your gun which killed Mrs Otterbourne, who was about to tell us who she believed killed both Linnet Doyle and the maid Louise—'

'Are you crazy?' Pennington shouted. 'What motive did I have to kill Linnet? Her money goes to her husband. *He* gets it all, not me.'

Race said: 'Mr Doyle never left the observation room that evening until he was shot in the leg. The doctor and the nurse both say that he couldn't walk a step afterwards. Simon Doyle could not have killed his wife. He could not have killed Louise Bourget. He certainly did not kill Mrs Otterbourne – I was there!'

'I know he didn't kill her. All I'm saying is, why do you think *I* killed her? I don't get any money from her death.'

'But, my dear sir,' Poirot's voice was soft, 'as soon as Madame Doyle got home and took control of her money, she would have learned that you have been stealing from her. But now that her husband gets her money, *the whole thing is different*. You will find it easy to give him complicated documents, and to delay giving him any money.'

He saw Mr Pennington's shoulders fall.

'You don't understand! With luck, everything will be OK by the middle of June.'

'And I suppose,' said Poirot, 'you could not stop yourself from pushing the rock?'

'It was an accident! I fell against it.'

Poirot and Race said nothing.

Pennington suddenly stood. He moved towards the door.

'You have no evidence. And I didn't shoot her! You can't prove anything.'

CHAPTER 19

As the door closed behind Pennington, Poirot said: *'Pennington did not do it, Race!* He had the motive, he *tried* to do it with that rock. But he is too weak. Now, there are one or two things – that message, for example – that I want to be certain of. First, I would like to speak to Tim Allerton.'

Soon Tim Allerton joined them.

'Ah, Monsieur Allerton,' said Poirot. 'For the last three years, there have been some jewellery <u>robberies</u> worrying the police. The thieves take the real jewellery and leave false jewellery in its place. My friend, Chief Inspector Japp, believes that there are two thieves working together. One of these thieves, he believes, is Mademoiselle Joanna Southwood.

'Every one of the <u>victims</u> knew her, and she had been very close to each piece of jewellery. Japp believes that she makes drawings of the jewellery and has a copy made. Then the other thief takes the real piece of jewellery and leaves the copy. But Japp does not yet know who the second thief is.

'Recently, you mentioned that you had been at a party where one of these robberies had happened, and that you are the cousin of Mademoiselle Southwood. And you obviously did not like me being here.

'I believe that you came to Egypt because you heard that Madame Doyle would be here for her honeymoon. After she was murdered, we discovered that her pearls were missing. But then the pearls were returned, and they were *false* – because you had changed them.'

Tim Allerton's face was white.

'I believe that the real pearls, Monsieur Allerton, are in a rosary that hangs in your cabin. The beads on that rosary are very clever. They can open, and inside each bead is a pearl, stuck there with a special glue. Most police who search you will not touch a rosary. You knew that.'

There was a silence. Then Tim said quietly: 'You win.'

Poirot continued.

'On the night that Linnet Doyle died, someone saw you leave her cabin just after one in the morning. Was Madame Doyle alive or dead when you stole the pearls?'

Tim said: 'Monsieur Poirot, I don't know! I thought she was asleep.'

'Was there any smell of smoke? A gun leaves a smell of smoke.'

'I don't think so. Who saw me?'

'Rosalie Otterbourne. But she did not tell me. I am Hercule Poirot! *I do not need to be told.* When I asked her, she said, "*I didn't see anybody.*" But she lied.'

Tim said in a strange voice: 'She's an extraordinary girl.' Then he looked at Race.

'Well, sir, where do we go from here? I admit that I took the pearl necklace from Linnet's cabin. But not that Joanna Southwood had anything to do with it.'

Poirot rang the bell. 'I am going to ask Miss Otterbourne if she will come here for a minute.'

Rosalie came, with her eyes red from crying. She looked a little shocked when she saw Tim.

Poirot said, 'When I asked you this morning if you saw anyone on the starboard deck, your answer was that you did not. Now, Monsieur Allerton has admitted that he was in Linnet Doyle's cabin last night.'

Rosalie looked at Tim.

'But you didn't – you didn't—?'

'No, I didn't kill her. I was stealing her pearl necklace.'

Poirot said, 'Monsieur Allerton's story is that he went to her cabin and put a necklace of false pearls in place of the real ones.'

'I—'

Tim began to speak but Poirot held up his hand.

'But Monsieur Allerton, I have not yet looked at the rosary in your cabin. It may be that, when I do, *I shall find nothing there.* And since Mademoiselle Otterbourne says that she saw no one on the deck last night – well, there is no evidence against you at all. The pearl necklace was taken by someone who has now returned it. The pearls are in a little box on the table by the door.'

Tim stood for a moment, unable to speak. Then, 'Thanks!' he said. 'You won't have to give me another chance!'

He held the door open for the girl; she went out and, picking up the little box, he followed her.

Outside, Tim took the false pearl necklace from the box and threw it into the Nile.

'There! When I return the box to Poirot the real pearl necklace will be in it. What a fool I've been!'

Rosalie said quietly: 'Why did you do it?'

'Oh, I was bored – I did it for the fun of it.'

'I think I understand.'

'Yes, but you wouldn't ever do it.'

'No,' she said. 'I wouldn't.'

He said: 'Oh, my dear, you're so lovely. Why didn't you say you'd seen me last night?'

'I thought they might <u>suspect</u> you.'

'Did *you* suspect me?'

'No. I couldn't believe that you'd kill anyone.'

He took her hand in his.

'Rosalie, would you… Would you ever be able to forget this awful thing I've done?'

She smiled at him. 'I'm not perfect either, Mr Allerton…'

Some minutes later, Tim said, 'I'm going to tell my mother everything. She's strong enough to know the truth.'

They went to Mrs Allerton's cabin and Tim knocked loudly on the door. Mrs Allerton opened it.

'Mother, Rosalie and I—' began Tim.

Then he paused, thinking about what to say next.

'Oh, my dears!' said Mrs Allerton. She took Rosalie in her arms. 'My dear, dear child, I always hoped – but Tim just <u>pretended</u> he didn't like you. But of course *I knew*!'

Rosalie cried happily.

CHAPTER 20

Colonel Race was looking serious.

'Poirot, I really cannot wait any longer! *Do* you know who killed the three victims on this boat or *don't* you?'

'I do. I am just about to tell you.'

There was a knock on the door. Race made an annoyed sound. It was Dr Bessner and Cornelia.

'Oh, Colonel Race,' said Cornelia, 'Miss Bowers has just told me about Cousin Marie and her little problem with taking things that aren't hers. It's been the most awful shock. But Dr Bessner has been wonderful, explaining how some people really can't help it.'

Poirot smiled at Cornelia before turning to the doctor. 'And how is your patient?'

'He's doing very well.'

Race said: 'Good. Then I can come along to your room and continue our conversation. He was telling me about a message.'

'It was very funny, that! Doyle tells me it was a message all about vegetables!'

Race said. 'So that's it! Richetti!'

He looked round at three confused faces.

'It was a <u>code</u> used in South Africa. Potatoes mean guns, carrots are bombs and so on. That means Richetti is a very dangerous man who's killed more than once. And he knew that if I heard Mrs Doyle repeat what was in that message, it would be the end for him!'

He turned to Poirot. 'Is Richetti the man?'

'He is *your* man,' said Poirot. 'But it was not Richetti who killed Linnet Doyle.'

Cornelia cried out: 'But who is it? Aren't you going to tell us?'

'*Mais oui* – of course,' Poirot said. 'I waited until now because I like an audience. I like everyone to say, "See how clever Hercule Poirot is!"'

'Well,' Race said gently, 'you have an audience now. So just how clever *is* Hercule Poirot?'

'To begin with, I was very stupid. The problem was Jacqueline de Bellefort's gun. Why was that gun not left at the place of the crime when the murderer wanted us to believe it was her? But the reason was very simple. The murderer *had* to take it away.

'You and I, my friend,' Poirot spoke to Race, 'started to investigate with the idea that the crime was a quick decision. But it was not. This crime was very carefully planned, with all the details worked out – they even put pills in my bottle of wine to make me sleep!

'Oh yes! I was put to sleep so that I could not possibly see anything that happened that night. I drink wine; the other people at my table do not. There is nothing easier than to slip a sleeping pill into my bottle of wine.

'I first knew this crime had been carefully planned when the gun was found in the Nile. It was wrapped in a velvet shawl. *If a gun is shot through velvet, it does not leave a burn on the victim's skin.* Therefore, the <u>shot</u> fired through the shawl *could not have been the shot that killed Linnet Doyle.* A *third* shot had been fired – but only two shots had been fired from the gun.

'The next interesting point was that in Linnet Doyle's cabin I found two bottles of nail polish. Linnet Doyle's nails had always been the colour called *Cardinal*, a deep dark red. The other bottle was labelled *Rose*. Rose is a pale pink colour, but the few drops still in the bottle were a bright red and smelled different than usual. That made me think that it was in fact *red ink*. I thought of the stained handkerchief which had been wrapped round the gun. Red ink washes out quickly but always stains material pale pink.

'I do not know why I did not see the truth at that moment, but then an event happened that left no doubt. Louise Bourget was killed by the murderer, because she was asking for money to stay quiet. When I asked her if she had seen anything the previous night, she gave this very strange answer: "*If* I had been unable to sleep, *if* I had climbed the stairs, *then* perhaps I might have seen the murderer…"

'Now what exactly did that tell us?'

Bessner replied quickly: 'It told you that she *had* climbed the stairs?'

'No, no, it is not that simple – why would she say that *to us*?

'There can be only one reason! She is saying it to the murderer, who she wishes to get money from; therefore *the murderer must have been present at the time*. But, besides myself and Colonel Race, only two people were there – Simon Doyle and Dr Bessner.

'Simon Doyle never left the observation room that evening before he was shot. And after that it was impossible for him to go to Madame Doyle's cabin.

'So Dr Bessner *must* be the guilty one. But then, my friends, a second fact became clear to me. Louise Bourget *could have spoken to Dr Bessner in private at any time*. So why in front of us? No, there was only one person who it could be – *Simon Doyle!* And remember his answer: "My good girl… I'll look after you." That was what she wanted to hear!'

'But I don't understand!' cried the doctor: 'It was *impossible* for Simon Doyle to leave his cabin.'

'I know,' said Poirot. 'So I looked again at the crime. What had actually been *seen*?

'Mademoiselle Robson had seen Mademoiselle de Bellefort fire her gun, had seen Simon Doyle fall, had seen him hold a handkerchief to his leg and had seen that handkerchief turn red. What had Monsieur Fanthorp heard and seen? He heard a shot, he found Doyle with a red-stained handkerchief held to his leg. Then what happened? Doyle insisted that Mademoiselle de Bellefort be taken away and not left alone.

'But the truth is that Doyle was not hurt at all. Mademoiselle Jacqueline did not hit him on purpose – and he is now alone for the next five minutes while Mademoiselle Robson and Monsieur Fanthorp are busy, *on the port side of the deck.*

'Simon Doyle picks up the gun from under the sofa, takes off his shoes, runs very quietly along the starboard deck, enters his wife's cabin, and shoots her in the head. He puts the bottle that contained the red ink on her table (it must not be found on him) and runs back. Then he gets out Mademoiselle Van Schuyler's shawl, which he has kept hidden, wraps it round the gun and fires a bullet into his own leg. The shawl hides the sound of the gun. He is lying by a window, so that he can open the window and throw the gun (with the handkerchief in the velvet shawl) into the Nile.'

'Impossible!' said Race. 'No man could work all that out so quickly, and certainly not someone like Doyle who is slow in his thinking.'

'True, but between the two of them, you get all the qualities needed – Jacqueline de Bellefort's calm, clever, planning brain, and Simon Doyle, the man who can do what needs to be done.

'What gave *Simon* his alibi?' continued Poirot. 'The shot fired by *Jacqueline*. What gave Jacqueline *her* alibi? *Simon's* demand that a hospital nurse must stay all night with her.

'Simon Doyle and Jacqueline were in love before. When you realize that they are still in love, it is suddenly all clear. Simon kills his rich wife, gets her money, *and after some time will marry his old love.* Jacqueline following Madame Doyle is all part of the plan. During that conversation I had with Jacqueline when she pretended that somebody was listening, *I* saw no one, because there *was* no one! She used it as a useful <u>red herring</u> later.

'The final drama was perfectly planned and timed. They gave me a pill to make me sleep, then they chose Mademoiselle Robson as a <u>witness</u>. Jacqueline says she has shot Doyle, Mademoiselle Robson says so, Monsieur Fanthorp says so, and when the doctor looks at Simon's leg – later on – he *has* been shot.

'And then the plan goes wrong. Louise Bourget has seen Simon Doyle run to his wife's cabin and come back. She understands what has happened. And so she asks for money.'

'But Mr Doyle couldn't have killed *her*? He was very ill in bed,' Cornelia said.

'No. Simon Doyle asks to see Jacqueline, asks me to leave them alone together. He then tells her of the new danger. He knows where Bessner's knives are. After the crime, the knife is cleaned and returned. Then, very late, Jacqueline de Bellefort comes in to lunch.

'But their problems continue: *Madame Otterbourne has seen Jacqueline go into Louise Bourget's cabin.* And she comes to tell Simon about it. Do you remember how Simon shouted at the poor woman? He was upset and ill, we thought. But no, he was trying to tell Jacqueline, who was in her cabin two doors down, that they were in danger. She heard – and acted as quick as lightning. She remembered that Pennington had talked about a gun, and his room was just next door. She found it, and fired.

'She only had to throw down the gun and run back to her cabin. It was a risk, but it was their only option.'

'What happened to the first bullet fired at Doyle by Jacqueline?' Race asked.

'I think it went into the table. There is a hole there. Doyle had time to dig it out with a knife and throw it through the window. He also had, of course, another bullet, so that it would look like only two shots had been fired.'

'They thought of everything,' Cornelia said. 'It's horrible!'

Poirot's eyes seemed to be saying: 'You are wrong. They did not consider Hercule Poirot.'

Aloud he said, 'And now, Doctor, we will go and speak to your patient...'

CHAPTER 21

Later that evening, Hercule Poirot sat with Jacqueline de Bellefort.

The girl spoke first.

'Well,' she said, 'I can't see much evidence, Monsieur Poirot. I don't believe it would convince a judge. But dear Simon, he just admitted everything, poor lamb.'

'And what about you, Mademoiselle?'

She laughed.

'Don't worry, Monsieur Poirot! About me, I mean. You do worry, don't you?'

'Yes, Mademoiselle.'

'But you still thought I should be punished?'

Hercule Poirot said quietly, 'Yes.'

She nodded her head. 'And you're quite right. I might do it again... It's so easy, killing people. You begin to feel that it doesn't matter, that only *you* matter! That's a dangerous feeling. Would you like to hear everything? From the beginning? You see, Simon and I loved each other...'

Poirot said: 'And for you, love was enough, but not for him.'

'You don't understand Simon. You see, he likes all the things you get with money – horses and boats and sport. And he'd never had any of them. He wants things just as a child wants them.

'But he never tried to marry anybody rich. He wasn't that type. And then we met and fell in love, but we couldn't imagine when we'd be able to marry. You see, he'd lost his job. He tried to do something clever with other people's money and it all went wrong. Poor thing.'

Poirot said nothing.

'I thought of Linnet and her new country house, and I hurried to her for help. Monsieur Poirot, I loved Linnet. We were true friends, but she just decided she was going to get Simon.... That's the truth – and it's why I'm not really sorry about her, even now.

'Simon didn't care about her! But he liked the thought of her money. I said that he should go and marry Linnet. But he said his idea of having money was to have it himself, not to have a rich wife controlling it. And he didn't want anyone but me...

'He said one day: "If I had any luck, I would marry her and she would die in a year and leave me all her money." And a strange look came into his eyes. That was when he first thought of it...

'Then, one day, I found him reading about <u>arsenic</u>. And I was frightened. Because, you see, *I knew he'd never manage it*. He's got no imagination. He would probably just put arsenic into her and think the doctor would say she died of a stomach ache.

'So I had to help, to look after him...'

Poirot had no doubt that this was all true. She had loved Simon Doyle too much.

'I thought and I thought and we worked out the details, little by little. I was glad that I didn't have to kill her. I could have killed her face to face, but not the other way...

'We planned it all so carefully. Even then, Simon wrote a J in blood which was a silly thing to do. But really it all went as we had planned.'

'Yes. It was not your fault that Louise Bourget could not sleep that night... And afterwards, Mademoiselle?'

'Yes,' she said. 'It's terrible, isn't it? I can't believe that I – I did that! I know now what you meant by evil coming into your heart... Louise made it clear to Simon that she knew. Simon told me what I had to do. I was so afraid... But Simon and I were safe except for this awful French girl. I took her all the money we had, pretending to be worried. And then, when she was counting the money, I did it! It was easy. That's what's so horribly, horribly frightening about it... It was so, so easy...

'But Mrs Otterbourne saw me. She came looking for you and I killed her so quickly. I knew it was life or death for us[5] – that seemed to make it better...'

She looked at his face, which looked terribly sad. She said gently:

'Don't worry about me, Monsieur Poirot. I was nearly very happy. However, this is how it is now.' She looked over towards the crew member standing by the door. 'I suppose he's here to make sure that I don't kill myself. I won't do that. It will be easier for Simon if I'm with him...'

CHAPTER 22

It was sunrise when they came into Shellal.

'Doyle deserves to die[5],' said Race. 'He's a cold-blooded murderer. I'm sorry for Miss de Bellefort, but we can't help her now.'

Poirot shook his head.

'Women who care for men the way Jacqueline cares for Doyle are very dangerous. It is what I said when I first saw them together. "She cares too much for him." It is true.'

Cornelia Robson came up beside him. 'I've been with Jacqueline. I felt it was awful to leave her alone in that room.'

Miss Van Schuyler was coming along the deck towards them.

'Cornelia, I think I will send you straight home.'

'I'm sorry, Cousin Marie, but I'm not going home. I'm going to get married.'

Ferguson came round the corner of the deck. He said: 'Cornelia, what's this I hear? It's not true!'

'It is true,' said Cornelia. 'I'm going to marry Dr Bessner. He asked me last night.'

'And why are you going to marry him?' said Ferguson angrily. 'Because he's rich?'

'No,' said Cornelia. 'I like him. He's kind, and he knows a lot. I'll have a wonderful life with him.'

'He's too fat,' said Mr Ferguson in a nasty voice.

'Well, I've got round shoulders,' replied Cornelia. 'What someone looks like doesn't matter. He says I could really help him with his work, and he's going to teach me lots of things.'

She moved away.

Ferguson said to Poirot: 'She prefers that old fool to me? The girl's mad!'

Poirot smiled.

'She is a woman with her own ideas,' he said.

The boat came in to the jetty.

Richetti, dark-faced, was taken off the boat by two of the crew. Then Simon Doyle was carried out, silent and frightened.

Jacqueline de Bellefort followed, a crew member beside her. She looked the same as usual. She came up to Simon.

'Hello, Simon!'

He looked up at her quickly. He looked happy again for a moment.

'I'm sorry, Jackie,' he said.

She smiled at him.

'It's all right, Simon,' she said. 'It was a fool's game, and we lost. That's all.'

She stopped to do up her shoe. Then suddenly, there was something in her hand.

There was a sharp *pop*.

Simon Doyle's body jumped, then did not move again.

Jacqueline de Bellefort stood for a moment, gun in hand, and smiled at Poirot.

As Race jumped forward, she turned the little gun against her heart and pressed the trigger.

She fell to the ground, dead. Race shouted: 'Where did she get that gun?'

Poirot felt a hand on his arm. Mrs Allerton said quietly, 'You knew?'

'She had a pair of these guns. I knew when I heard that one had been found in Rosalie Otterbourne's handbag the day of the search. Jacqueline sat at the same table as the Otterbournes. When she heard that there was going to be a search, she put the gun into Rosalie's handbag. Later, she went to Rosalie's cabin and got it back while they talked about makeup.'

'Why didn't you say? Did you want her to choose to kill herself?'

'Yes. But I knew that she would not choose it for herself alone. And so Simon Doyle has died an easier death than he deserved.'

Mrs Allerton said sadly: 'Love can be a very frightening thing.'

Then she noticed Tim and Rosalie, standing in the sun, and said suddenly and very happily:

'But, <u>thank goodness</u>, there *is* happiness in the world.'

'As you say, Madame, thank goodness.'

◆ CHARACTER LIST ◆

Joanna Southwood: a young, rich English woman; friend of Linnet Ridgeway and cousin of Tim Allerton

Linnet Ridgeway: a very rich and beautiful 20-year-old woman

Jacqueline de Bellefort: Linnet's school friend, whose parents lost all their money

Hercule Poirot: a very famous Belgian detective, who lives in England

Simon Doyle: a handsome but poor young Englishman who has to work for money

Mrs Allerton: an English woman on a Nile tour with her son

Tim Allerton: Mrs Allerton's son. Although the Allertons are no longer very rich, Tim doesn't have to work for money

Rosalie Otterbourne: English girl on a Nile Tour with her mother, a famous writer

Mrs Otterbourne: Rosalie's mother, a writer

Guido Richetti: An Italian archaeologist

Miss Marie Van Schuyler: A rich elderly American

Cornelia Robson: Miss Van Schuyler's young cousin

Miss Bowers: Miss Van Schuyler's nurse

Dr Bessner: a middle-aged Austrian doctor

Jim Fanthorp: a young English lawyer

Mr Ferguson: a young Englishman with Communist beliefs

Andrew Pennington: an American lawyer, responsible for Linnet's money until she is 21 or married

Colonel Race: a British Intelligence officer who knows Poirot

Louise Bourget: French, maid to Linnet

Mr Fleetwood: an English engineer on the Nile steamer, the *Karnak*

◆ CULTURAL NOTES ◆

1. The British class system

In 1937, when *Death on the Nile* was written, Britain had a class system with rules that everybody knew and most people followed. People were upper, middle or working class. *Joanna Southwood*'s title 'The Honourable' tells us that she is a member of the upper class. They usually did not work. Many families still owned land and were rich, but others had lost their money but still tried to have a rich lifestyle. Some stayed with one rich friend and then another, like Joanna with Linnet.

The middle classes were educated people who had to work for their money – they had professions in the law (like *Jim Fanthorp*), medicine (like *Dr Bessner*), education, business, the Church or something similar.

People were expected to have friends and marry someone belonging to the same social class, but some upper class people did marry very rich business people.

This class system lasted until the Second World War (1939–1945) when many social rules changed, especially the role of women in society.

2. Country houses and estates

Rich people often had large houses in the country, such as Linnet's property, Wode Hall. These houses had a lot of land that often included villages and farms. All the land together was called the estate. Each estate had a land agent who looked after the estate for the owner. In this story, Jacqueline asks Linnet to make *Simon Doyle* her land agent at Wode Hall.

3. Maids

In England at this time, the upper classes employed servants. Ladies usually had a personal servant called a maid, such as *Louise Bourget*, whose main job was to keep the lady's clothes and accessories clean and ready to wear. They also helped their mistresses get dressed, change clothes for meals or activities and to get ready for bed at night. However, by the end of the Second World War, this situation was starting to change.

4. Touring in Egypt in 1937 *(see also map on page 85)*

When *Death on the Nile* was first published in 1937, only the very rich could afford to travel abroad for pleasure. They would arrive in the capital city of Cairo and be led by a guide to a number of places, from the Pyramids just near to Cairo, then down the River Nile to explore the city of Aswan, Elephantine Island and some of the most beautiful temples built by the Ancient Egyptians like the rock temples at Abu Simbel. They would also visit natural wonders such as the First and Second Cataracts, areas of the Nile where the water is not deep enough for a boat and there are lots of large rocks.

Rich tourists in Egypt would travel in luxury, on large steamboats where they had a cabin each and a formal dinner every evening.

5. The death penalty

When *Death on the Nile* was first published in 1937, the consequences of murder in the UK were different from today. If you killed a person on purpose, you could be punished for the crime by death. This was called the death penalty. The government ended the death penalty for murder in the UK in 1965.

6. The British Intelligence Service

The British Intelligence Service is an organization designed to keep Britain safe by secretly getting information (called intelligence) about what other countries or people are doing that might be dangerous for Britain. *Colonel Race* works for the British Intelligence Service.

7. Franc

The franc was the name of the money used in France up until the introduction of the euro on 1 January 1999.

8. Eton

Eton is a famous independent boys' school in Britain. It is very expensive. Many of Britain's prime ministers, politicians, judges and top army people went to Eton. Prince William and his brother, Prince Harry, were educated there. Men who went to Eton often wear their old school ties as a sign of their position in society.

Route of the *Karnak* in 1937

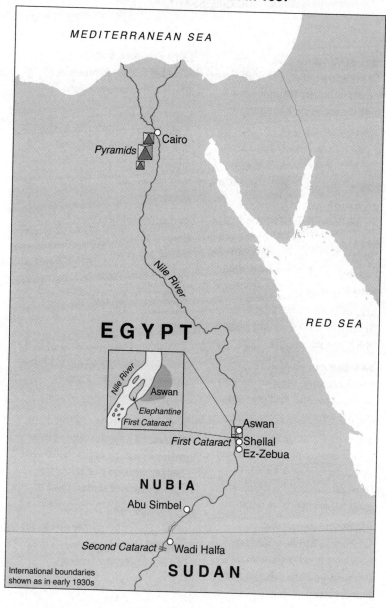

◆ Glossary ◆

accept TRANSITIVE VERB
To **accept** a difficult or unpleasant situation means to understand that it cannot be changed.

alibi COUNTABLE NOUN
If you have an **alibi**, you can prove that you were somewhere else when a crime was committed.

archaeologist COUNTABLE NOUN
An **archaeologist** studies societies and people of the past by examining what is left of their buildings and the objects they used to use.

arsenic UNCOUNTABLE NOUN
Arsenic is a very strong poison which can kill people.

bad-tempered ADJECTIVE
If you are **bad-tempered**, you are not cheerful and you get angry easily.

bead COUNTABLE NOUN
Beads are small pieces of glass, wood, or plastic with a hole through the middle which are used for jewellery or decoration.

blush INTRANSITIVE VERB
When you **blush**, your face becomes redder than usual because you are ashamed or embarrassed.

bullet COUNTABLE NOUN
A **bullet** is a small piece of metal which is fired from a gun.

capitalist ADJECTIVE
A **capitalist** country or system is one in which business, and industry are owned by private individuals and not by the government.

carve TRANSITIVE VERB
If you **carve** an object, you cut it out of stone or wood.

case COUNTABLE NOUN
A **case** is a crime that the police are working on.

cliff COUNTABLE NOUN
A **cliff** is a high area of land with a very steep side, especially one next to the sea.

code COUNTABLE NOUN
A **code** is a system of replacing the words in a message with other words or symbols, so that people who do not know the system cannot understand it.

cold-blooded ADJECTIVE
If you describe someone as **cold-blooded**, you mean they do not show any feelings.

colonel COUNTABLE NOUN
A **colonel** is a senior person in the army, navy or air force.

conceited ADJECTIVE
If you say that someone is **conceited**, you feel that they are far too proud of their abilities or achievements.

consequences PLURAL NOUN
The **consequences** of something are the results or effects of it.

darling VOCATIVE NOUN
You call someone **darling** if you love them or like them very much.

deceive TRANSITIVE VERB
If you **deceive** someone, you make them believe something that is not true.

deck COUNTABLE NOUN
The **deck** of a ship is a floor outside which you can walk on.

evidence UNCOUNTABLE NOUN
Evidence is information which is used to prove that something is true.

evil UNCOUNTABLE NOUN
Evil is used to refer to all the wicked and bad things that happen in the world.

false ADJECTIVE
If something is **false**, it is incorrect or not true.

guilty secret PHRASE
A **guilty secret** is something that only you know and knowing it makes you feel guilty or bad.

handkerchief COUNTABLE NOUN
A **handkerchief** is a small square of fabric which you use for blowing your nose.

hesitate INTRANSITIVE VERB
If you **hesitate**, you pause slightly while you are doing something or just before you do it, usually because you do not know what to do, or you are, embarrassed, or worried.

in the dark PHRASE
If you are **in the dark** about something, you do not know anything about it.

investigate TRANSITIVE VERB
If someone, especially a police officer, **investigates** an event or a crime, they try to find out what happened or what is the truth.

jetty COUNTABLE NOUN
A **jetty** is a wide wooden or stone wall or wooden platform where boats stop to let people get on and off, or to take goods on and off boats.

let down PHRASAL VERB
If you **let** someone **down**, you disappoint them, usually by not doing something that you said you would do.

motive COUNTABLE NOUN
Your **motive** for doing something is your reason for doing it.

nail polish VARIABLE NOUN
Nail polish is a thick liquid that women paint on their nails.

nod INTRANSITIVE VERB
If you **nod**, you move your head down and up to show that you understand or like something, or that you agree with it.

parasol COUNTABLE NOUN
A **parasol** is an object like an umbrella that provides shade from the sun.

pearl ADJECTIVE
Pearl is used to describe something, especially jewellery, that is hard, shiny and white. Pearls come from the inside of a seashell.

pretend TRANSITIVE VERB
If you **pretend** that something is true, you try to make people believe that it is true, although it is not.

red herring COUNTABLE NOUN
If you say that something is a **red herring**, you mean that it is not important and it takes your attention away from the main subject or problem you are considering.

reputation COUNTABLE NOUN
To have a **reputation** for something means to be known or remembered for it.

risk COUNTABLE NOUN
If something that you do is a **risk**, it might have unpleasant results.

robbery VARIABLE NOUN
Robbery is the crime of stealing money or other objects.

rosary COUNTABLE NOUN
A **rosary** is a string of beads that members of some religions use for counting prayers.

shake one's head PHRASE
If you **shake your head**, you move it from side to side in order to say 'no'.

shawl COUNTABLE NOUN
A **shawl** is a large piece of woollen cloth worn over a woman's shoulders or head.

shot COUNTABLE NOUN
If you fire a **shot**, you fire a gun once.

silly ADJECTIVE
Someone who is being **silly** is behaving in a way that may make other people laugh at them.

slave COUNTABLE NOUN
A **slave** is a person who is owned by another person and has to work for that person without pay.

splash COUNTABLE NOUN
A **splash** is the sound made when something hits or falls into water.

stab TRANSITIVE VERB
If someone **stabs** another person, they push a knife into their body.

stain TRANSITIVE VERB
If a liquid **stains** something, the thing becomes coloured or marked by the liquid.

steamer COUNTABLE NOUN
A **steamer** is a ship that is powered by steam.

suspect COUNTABLE NOUN
A **suspect** is a person who the police think may be guilty of a crime.
TRANSITIVE VERB
If you **suspect** someone of doing something that is not honest or is unpleasant, you believe that they probably did it.

temple COUNTABLE NOUN
A **temple** is a building used for the worship of a god or gods in certain religions.

terrace COUNTABLE NOUN
A **terrace** is a flat area of stone or grass next to a building where people can sit.

thank goodness PHRASE
You say **thank goodness** when you are very happy that something bad has not happened.

threat COUNTABLE NOUN
A **threat** is something unpleasant that someone says they will do, especially if you do not do what they want.

title COUNTABLE NOUN
Someone's **title** is a word such as 'Lord' or 'Mrs' that is used before their name to show their status or profession.

trigger COUNTABLE NOUN
The **trigger** of a gun is the part which you pull to make it work.

trustee COUNTABLE NOUN
A **trustee** is someone with legal control of money or property that is kept or invested for another person.

unacceptable ADJECTIVE
If you describe something as **unacceptable**, you are very unhappy about it and feel that it should not be allowed to happen.

velvet UNCOUNTABLE NOUN
Velvet is soft cloth that is thick on one side.

victim COUNTABLE NOUN
A **victim** is someone who has been hurt or killed by someone or something.

witness COUNTABLE NOUN
A **witness** to an event such as an accident or crime is a person who saw it.